HER ALIEN FORGEMASTERS

SUSAN HAYES

SUSAN HAYES

Her Alien Forgemasters (Book 3 of the Drift: Haven Colony)

First Print & E-book Publication: October 2021

Editor: Amanda Brown

Published by: Black Scroll Publications Ltd.

DEDICATION

For my Mum and Dad, for all their love and support.

ABOUT THE BOOK

She doesn't do mornings, cardio, or long-term relationships. Then her mates walked into her bar...

Anya couldn't be happier. Her tavern is packed every night, her staff is amazing, and her nosy mother is busy hauling cargo on the far side of the galaxy. It's taken her years of work to reach this moment, and she's ready to relax and enjoy the ride.

The last thing she needs is a romance to mess up her plans. She's managed quite well without a man in her life, so why did the universe send her *two*?

He'd always known they'd find their destined mate. He just never imagined she'd be *human*.

Tra'var loves his new life. Haven colony isn't perfect, but it's far better than the unchanging, inflexible society they left behind. Here everyone is free to be themselves.

All that's missing is the female who will complete their triad and forge them into the family he's always dreamed of... but he wasn't prepared for Anya. She wasn't anything like he'd expected, even if she might be everything they need.

He's been an outcast his whole life... what female would ever want him?

Damos can transform ordinary steel into anything from weapons to ornaments, but he'll never be able to change the one thing he truly wishes he could... himself.

Born flawed in a society where genetic perfection is the standard, he's only been tolerated but never accepted. Haven might be different. But when Anya learns the truth, will she see past his flaws and embrace him as her mate?

PROLOGUE

BEYOND THE EDGE of civilized space is a newly colonized planet. It's a haven for the homeless, the hopeful, and those dreaming of freedom.

The beings who live here might be different species from vastly different worlds - but they all have one thing in common. Whoever they are, and wherever they came from, Haven is now their home.

The land is uncharted. The dangers are unknown. It's a world full of possibilities – for those willing to risk everything.

Welcome to Haven Colony.

1

———

Tra'var glanced out the window of their domicile and then did a double take. Snow? That hadn't been in the forecast.

"I'm going out back to make sure the forge is secure. It's snowing!"

Damos grunted from his bedroom but didn't make an appearance. "Great. Then we don't need to go out. I'll give you a hand and then we can pour our own drinks here and let Striker know we're snowed in."

"Not happening. We. Are. Going. I don't care if there's a blizzard. We promised we'd be there to celebrate." There was a party for Striker and Maggie tonight to mark their mating and Maggie's status as the colony's newest citizen. Since he and his *anrik* had played a large part in rescuing Maggie from her abductors, Striker had sicced his female on Damos until the big, grumpy male had finally agreed to attend.

"Striker will understand. That male likes parties even less than we do." Damos finally emerged from his room. Despite his grumbling, he was dressed for an evening out. His hair was neatly tied back, his jaw recently shaved. He'd donned polished boots, pants that had never been near enough to the forge to be damaged or singed, and a collared vest that Tra'var had never seen before.

"I didn't know you owned anything without burn marks."

His *anrik* flipped an obscene gesture at him. "I didn't. But they have these things called shops. You go there and buy things you don't have."

"I'm familiar with the concept. I wasn't aware you were." Tra'var pulled on a jacket, arranging the long, heavy garment so his wings could be extended through slits in the back if needed.

"I do leave the house occasionally."

"Very occasionally, which is counter to our whole reason for coming here." They'd signed up for the new colony within hours of the announcement as a chance to start over somewhere new. A place where everyone would be judged on their own merits and not on their bloodlines was exactly what they needed.

At least, that was the plan. The reality was more complicated. Not everyone had left the old ways behind. There was still some bias and posturing. Wariness too. It would take time to discover the shape this new colony would take. Tra'var was hopeful. Damos was less so. Getting him out for a night with their new friends would be a major milestone. It would also be a step toward putting their mark on this place. If they wanted change, they needed to be present to make it happen.

Besides, he was sick of his *anrik's* company. They might be blood-brothers, but if they spent one more night drinking ale and talking shop, Tra'var might just start throwing things. Given their home was also their storefront for the weapons they made, that had the potential to get messy.

Damos donned his jacket and pulled up the hood. "If we're doing this, we better get going. The sooner we arrive, the sooner we can leave."

"You agreed to two drinks and a meal," he reminded Damos.

Another grunt. "I did. I'm still not sure how that happened. Maggie haggles better than half the traders we've ever done business with."

"I noticed. Next time we have to negotiate prices for *tarchozin*, do you think we could borrow her?"

Damos nodded thoughtfully. "That's not a bad idea. She's very good. I don't even know what I agreed to exactly, except that we have to try something called 'Almost Heaven' and Maggie's signature cocktail. I think it was called an Aftershock? After... something. My head was spinning by that point." Damos paused at the door and turned back to face Tra'var, though his face was shadowed by his hood. "I don't know if I should feel sorry for Striker or envy him."

"I envy him. He found his *mahaya*. The fact she is

a match for him in every way is his own fault for being such a stubborn, growly male."

Damos was halfway out the door before he spoke again. "Then it's a good thing we haven't found ours. I cannot imagine what kind of female the ancestors would send us."

Tra'var didn't answer. He flipped up his own hood and followed his *anrik* outside, his mind full of images of what their mate would be like. Soft. Smiling. Gentle enough to soothe the scars in Damos' psyche and fill their home with light and laughter. One day, they would find her. They had to. As they aged, the urge to seek out their mate only grew stronger. If they didn't find her soon, they could begin the transition to *onar*, those who had failed to find their mate and were destined to spend their lives alone. It was an unpleasant experience, one not everyone survived with mind and body intact.

They needed to find their *mahaya* before that happened. Then they would be complete.

Damos wasn't sure how he felt about tonight, and he didn't like it. He preferred to be certain about things. The correct shape for a blade. What temperature the forge should be. When to quench a blade and call it complete. He understood these things. Social cues and the nuances of polite society were far more complicated, especially for an outsider like him. It was easier to avoid them altogether.

They made the walk from their home in what had become the artists' quarter to the broad bridge that linked the two sides of the colony. Flying would be faster, but the distance was beyond the range of what his imperfect wings could manage. They walked instead. Back on Vardaria Prime, that would have earned him pitying or scornful looks. He was flawed—an imperfect being in a society that valued lineage and breeding over ability and skill.

It wasn't the same here, but it wasn't easy to leave the old ways behind, either. Not for others and not for him.

The first snow of the season swirled around them, and he shoved his hands into his pockets before the chill triggered his scales to tighten. The natural armor was protection against attack, but it also made them resistant to heat and cold. In his case, though, it triggered more of the elements that made him different. His body didn't know the difference between a cold wind and a violent assault, and the last thing he wanted was to arrive at the Bar None tavern sporting talons on his hands and raised scales down his spine.

This wasn't the first time he'd been to the bridge that spanned the river. He'd crossed it a few times to make deliveries, but that had always been during daylight hours. The place looked different now. For one thing, it was quieter. The street vendors had packed up their stalls for the night. A few beings were out and about, but they had their heads down and walked with purpose.

It was easy to spot their destination. The tavern was well-lit and noisy enough, and the sound carried on the wind, filling the night with faint laughter and music.

They reached the entrance, both moving to one side of the door to bang the snow from their boots and shake out their coats. It was an old habit, and the pause gave Damos a few more seconds to ensure his more unusual features weren't in evidence. In a perfect world, he wouldn't have to worry about it, but Haven wasn't ready for that.

Neither was he.

They went inside. The first thing that struck him were the differences. This was not a Vardarian place. The walls were painted in dark shades and the furniture, while clearly mass-produced, wasn't all the same style. Some seating was built for smaller body frames, and others had no back, which was the preferred style for most of his kind.

The main room was large, but it still felt small to him. Only when he looked up did he understand why. Vardarian spaces had higher ceilings, space for the patrons to stretch their wings if needed. The ceiling here was low enough he had to suppress the urge to duck his head.

Bots scooted around the floor, carting drinks and food orders to tables and booths, most of which were full despite the weather. The bar was tended by a pair of droids, and electronic menus sat on every table. Good. He'd be able to order and get served without having to interact with anyone he didn't know.

They stripped off their coats and added them to the racks that lined the wall by the door before looking around for Striker and Maggie. The pair wasn't hard to spot. They were seated at the back of the room, surrounded by a group of familiar faces. Damos relaxed. He knew them all.

"They even saved us seats," Tra'var sent the subvocalized message directly to Damos' implanted receiver.

He just grunted in response. Maneuvering in the crowded space was tricky for someone of his dimensions, and the last thing he wanted was to bump someone and trigger an unwanted fight. It probably wouldn't happen here on Haven, but a lifetime of avoiding attention wasn't easy to move past.

They were only a few steps from the group when a scent brushed against his awareness. Something... delicious was in the air. He took another breath. Yes. There. Behind him. Achingly familiar yet entirely new, the scent called to him. He turned and inhaled deeply.

She was here.

"Tra'var. Taste the air and tell me what you sense." He was already scanning the room as he messaged his *anrik*, looking for the source of that elusive scent. Vardarian females were seated around the room but they weren't right. Cyborg females were present too,

but his gaze moved over them all until they landed on a solitary female behind the bar.

Behind it. Not seated at it. Was that the female who owned this tavern? The human? Forge and flame. Was their *mahaya* human?

He drew in another breath and arousal hit him like a speeding meteor. It was her.

Tra'var spun around. "Her?"

"Yes."

"She is beautiful," Tra'var said, his tone reverential.

"And human."

"Older," Tra'var said.

"And ours."

They walked toward her, barely noticing silence as the entire room watched this moment unfold.

They'd found her. Their *mahaya*. Their mate.

Anya had enjoyed a string of good days since coming to Haven, but this one was even better than usual. Her bar was packed, the patrons were all behaving, and everything was working the way it should.

The moment she had that thought, she rapped her knuckles three times on the top of the bar to ward off any bad luck that might be tempted by her open invitation to cause havoc. She'd had more than her share of chaos before coming here, and she had no doubt more would be in her future. Just... not right now. Tonight they all wanted to celebrate.

Every citizen of Haven knew the story of how this place had come to be and how many factions would like to see them fail. Torex Mining Corp wanted their planet back so they could tear it apart to reach the rich veins of tantalum buried beneath the surface. Darker forces wanted to reclaim their lost "property," the cyborgs they had imprisoned and experimented on in their mad quest to build a better soldier.

And then there were the Vardarians. Thousands of them had followed Prince Tyran to Haven to start a new life far from the boundaries of their empire. She didn't have to know the details to understand there was a reason so many beings uprooted their lives to travel across the stars and start their lives over again.

One thing she'd learned in her life was that beings were the same the galaxy over. It didn't matter what sect, class, or species they were, intelligent life all seemed to follow the same patterns. Most of them tried to be good, even if they often failed, and some of them always reached for more than they should have. Power, wealth, influence. When it reached a certain point, the decent ones always left and tried to start over somewhere new... and then the whole dance started over again.

That's what Haven was—the first steps in a dance that might end in a year, a decade, or a few millennia. There was no way to know, and that was part of the magic. All she could be certain of was that here and now was her best chance to be a part of something special. It's what Phaedra had offered her, along with the unvarnished truth about the challenges Anya would face if she came. Unstable cyborgs who distrusted humans, a new species no one knew much about, and a new world that hadn't even been surveyed properly.

She'd said yes in a heartbeat.

Now she had a booming business and a sense of community she'd never known before. These beings weren't just her customers. They were her friends and neighbors. And tonight, they'd gathered to celebrate the newest addition to their ranks. After being claimed by Striker, Maggie was now officially a citizen of Haven and the first of the human refugees to reach that status. As far as Anya was concerned, no one deserved happiness more than Maggie. It made her heart happy to hear her friend's laughter and watch her lean into Striker's side, her joy an almost tangible thing that lifted everyone around her.

"She glows," Saral said as she placed a plate of snacks in front of Anya. "It's nice to see."

"It is."

"So would seeing you eat. You work too hard and don't take care of yourself. You need to find a good male or two to make sure you are well cared for."

"That is your answer to everything. Males are not the cure to all the troubles of the universe."

"No. True. They are also the cause of many of them. But the orgasms help." Saral laughed and touched her hand. "You'll see when you meet your destiny."

"Bah. My destiny is to grow old and rich running this place, or one like it. Which won't happen if my best cook is out of the kitchen much longer. Shoo!"

The Vardarian female retreated to her domain again, still laughing softly. As happy as Saral was with her mates, she couldn't see that not everyone was destined for that kind of love. Some, like Anya, just didn't seem easy to love, and that was fine by her. She knew her flaws and accepted them because they were part of who she was. She'd been around long enough to learn to like the woman she'd become.

"And I don't have time for a man, anyway. I barely have time for me."

The droids had the orders covered, so she took her plate and retreated to the end of the bar to eat. Not long after, the door opened and two new faces walked into her bar. She'd never seen either of them before.

Single she might be, but she wasn't blind. If she'd laid eyes on either of these males before, she'd remember. They were both Vardarian, one silver-skinned and the other golden. The silver one was slightly taller than his companion, but the golden one was larger in general, a veritable mountain of a male nearly as broad as he was tall.

When they removed their coats, she got an eyeful of powerful shoulders and arms that dwarfed even the other Vardarians present. No arm bands either, which meant they were unmated. The taller one was blond with a broad smile and rugged features while the golden one kept his expression guarded and moved with care between the tables, avoiding even the slightest contact with the other patrons.

She knew the look. He was used to having to work to avoid trouble or notice, though with his size, she couldn't imagine who or what would dare to take issue with him.

They were almost to the back of the room where Maggie and Striker were holding court when the dark-haired one stopped and turned around. He took a deep breath, his massive chest rising as he sucked in a lungful of air.

Fraxx. She knew what that meant. The male had caught a scent that intrigued him. It might be the roasted *gharshtu* on special tonight, or it could mean he'd detected the scent of his mate.

When he started looking around the room, she knew dinner wasn't what had his interest.

"Here we go again." She watched, curious to see who it would be. Several Vardarian females were present tonight, along with a large group of cyborg women who were celebrating with Maggie. Who was about to have their lives turned upside down?

When the big male's gaze landed on her, she expected him to take one look and keep moving.

He didn't. His amber eyes brightened, and he took another breath.

Oh, hell no.

A second later, the blond spun around to stare at her, too.

Anya took a step back. This was not happening. She'd known when she agreed to come here that as a single female this was theoretically possible, but she'd never for one second thought she'd be some Vardarians' mate.

Both males stalked toward her, their skin gleaming like newly minted coins as their scales tightened, a sure sign they were agitated.

So was she.

"*Mahaya*," the blond one said, his voice a deep rumble.

"Ma-hay-nope," she retorted, stepping back from the bar to put more space between them. "I serve the food, but I am not on the menu."

"But you are our *mahaya*," the dark-haired one spoke this time, and his voice was pitched like rolling thunder.

Damn. He was sexy. They both were. If they'd been looking for a night of no-strings-attached sex, she might have been tempted. But this?

It had to be a mistake.

Both males stepped around to the opening at the end of the bar at the exact same moment. As they reached out to her, she noted they bore a matching pair of circular scars on their wrists. They were *anrik*, a blood-bonded pair.

"I can't be. There has to be a mistake."

"No mistake," the blond said. "I am Tra'var. This is my *anrik*, Damos. What is your name?"

"Anya. Anya Hutchinson."

"Anya." Damos spoke the word with all the intensity of a prayer. "Shining star. It suits you."

"It does?"

"Oh yes." Tra'var reached for her again.

"Come. We have a lot to discuss and not much time."

To her surprise, Anya stepped out from the bar and took their hands as if it was the most natural thing in the world to do. She was even smiling for *fraxx* sake, despite the fact that every sensible cell in her brain was screaming at her to run for the hills before it was too late.

"Finally!" Saral exclaimed from the kitchen door, her smile as bright as a binary star system. "Go with them, Anya. We'll take care of this place. You... enjoy yourself. Oh, your mother will be so pleased!"

"Do *not* tell my mother anything!" She didn't want or need Hezza to cut short her cargo run so she could stick her nose into Anya's business. If this was happening, the last thing in the galaxy she needed was her mother's help.

When it came to relationships, she didn't need anyone's help, especially not a woman who had more romantic shipwrecks in her past than anyone else in the galaxy. Anya had enough wreckage in her own past to know how this was likely to go. If past was prologue, plenty of evidence suggested she could screw this up all on her own.

2

Tra'var's mind was shattered. The pieces were scattered to the winds of chance... or more accurately, the whims of his ancestors.

Their *mayaha's* name was Anya, and she was human. He forced himself into a moment of calm and took a good look at her. Her dark red-brown hair was bound back in some sort of tight braid, and her scaleless skin was a pale shade of gold. She had a soft, curvy body, and the lines around her eyes deepened when she smiled.

Her smile was dazzling as he stared at her, entranced.

"We should go somewhere private," Damos said.

Anya cocked a brow and eyed them both, her hands swallowed up inside of theirs. "I know what the *sharhal* is and where this is heading. I'm not sure privacy is a good idea right now. We need to talk, not..." she trailed off.

"We have time. As much as you need." Even as he said it, Tra'var questioned if that was true. They'd only scented her moments ago and he could already feel the first effects of the *sharhal*—the mating fever. Agitation. Desire. His skin gleamed bright silver, an effect created when his scales tightened.

Scales... *qarf*.

He glanced over at Damos. His *anrik's* skin was as bright as molten gold. Fortunately, he'd unfolded his wings just enough to hide the changes to his back, and his fingers were carefully curled so his talons weren't visible. He wouldn't be comfortable until they were away from the others, though. He never was. Damos had never accepted his differences, and until he did, he couldn't believe anyone else would either.

"Where would you be comfortable?" Tra'var asked Anya.

The question caught her by surprise. "Um. We really can't talk here. Can we?" She looked around. They were still the center of attention.

"Go already!" a beaming Vardarian female called from the kitchen doorway. She was pointing up to the ceiling. Tra'var didn't understand what it meant, but Anya must have.

"Thank you. Now get back to work, you meddling female!" Anya called back in passable Vardarian.

Damos sent him a subvocalized message. "*She speaks our language. I didn't expect that.*"

"*She does.*" This female was already surprising them.

"Come with me." Anya tightened her grip on both their hands as she made her way to the front door, pausing just long enough to let them all collect their coats.

"We're going outside?" Damos asked.

"It's snowing out there," Tra'var warned her.

"Oh! Then this is an even better idea. Come on." The little female darted out the door without even donning her coat.

They shared a bewildered look and went after her. Wherever she was going, they would follow.

She stepped out into the snow and laughed, arms outstretched and her face tipped up to the sky. "So this is snow?"

"You've never experienced this before?" Damos asked.

"Never. I've spent time on planets before but always in resort locations—warm weather, beaches, places where beings would come to relax and enjoy themselves."

"That sounds like a nice way to grow up. My family is from the mountains. I stopped enjoying snow once I was old enough to be expected to help clear it away," Tra'var said.

"It gets that deep?" Anya looked around. For now, the blanket of snow was minimal. None of them knew exactly what winter would look like in this place because no one had been here before.

"It can." Damos placed his jacket over her shoulders. The garment was so big it swallowed up her entire body, the edge barely skimming above the snow.

"That'll take some getting used to, just like everything else about this place." Anya turned to smile at Damos, her hands on his coat, and Tra'var experienced a pang of jealousy. It was like a hot needle driven into his gut.

He was at her side before he even made a conscious decision to move. "You will have us to keep you warm."

Damos smirked. "Losing control already?"

Tra'var ignored the jibe. He wasn't going to admit that the *sharhal* was already making it difficult to stay rational and patient.

"Uh. Yeah. For the moment, that won't be necessary. We'll be out of the weather in a few minutes. This way." Anya was on the move before she finished speaking. She darted away again, leaving them to follow the tantalizing trail of her pheromones.

"She seems uneasy," Damos muttered.

"Two strangers just walked into her establishment and claimed she was their mate. If I were in her place, I'd be skittish, too."

Damos held out his hand, revealing the claws he'd been struggling to hide. "True. Still. You should probably go first."

"I will not. You outrank me, Damos Arosa. You will go first and I will follow." Tra'var inclined his head. "It is the way things are."

Damos snorted. "The only time you say that is when you think it will provide you an advantage."

"That is your fault. You're so *qarfing* stubborn nothing else works." He pushed his *anrik* in the direction Anya had gone. "If we don't move quickly, she's going to think we don't want to be with her."

"If she believes that, she doesn't understand the *sharhal*." Damos grinned so broadly his fangs showed. "Shall we clarify things for her?"

It was the happiest Tra'var had seen him since the day they'd left Vardaria behind. By all the winds that blew, this was a good day.

Perhaps the best day they'd ever had.

Anya climbed the flight of stairs, keeping a firm grip on the railing to avoid slipping on the icy steps. She'd need to sweep them off in the morning and then find some way to keep them free of ice and snow. She had no idea what that entailed, but she'd ask around.

"'Oh, the climate is mild,' she said. 'The odds of you being the mate to any of the Vardarians is smaller than a Jeskyran's junk,' she said." She made it to the top of the stairs just as the two males reached the first step. "That is the last time I trust Phaedra *fraxxing* Kari."

Still, she couldn't help but appreciate the view as the two males ascended the stairs. They were striking in every way she could think of, including a few that had her normally slumbering libido perk up and take notice.

They were only halfway to her when she was struck by a totally irrational urge to go back down the icy steps just so she could be with them sooner.

Great. Five minutes after first contact and her brain was already starting to melt into slag. What would she be like in an hour... or a week? She thought about Saral and the shameless, joyful way she interacted with her mates even after all these years.

So... maybe it wouldn't be all bad. But that depended on who her mates turned out to be. She knew their names and species. That wasn't a lot to go on.

They really needed to talk.

Damos arrived first and she stepped aside to give him space to join her on the patio. It was protected from the elements by a small shield like the ones the Vardarians used to weatherproof the massive practice arena and parts of the other public spaces. There were plans to eventually cover the entire bridge with one. They'd have to move up the timeline now the weather had changed or the businesses that operated here would be hard pressed to stay open.

Anya knew she was distracting herself with thoughts of business instead of dealing with her more pressing concern—the two males now looking around with interest.

"You live here?" Tra'var asked, nodding toward the door leading inside her apartment.

"I do. The downstairs neighbors are kind of noisy, but the commute is the fastest in town."

Damos chuckled. "Not as fast as ours. We don't need to use stairs. We have wings."

"You work out of your home, too?" She gestured to a pair of chairs. "Actually, don't answer that just yet. Have a seat. I thought we could talk out here and watch the snow fall. It's prettier than I expected, and once I open the door this space heats up quickly.

The two males shared a glance. "You don't want us inside your home?" Damos' words were even, but she saw the way his expression tightened.

Veth. She was going to have to be honest and hope it didn't do more damage. "Honestly? No. Because I am already experiencing the first effects of whatever weirdness this is, and I don't trust myself to make good choices right now. All I know about you are your names."

"Would it be easier if you spent time with only one of us? I could go and leave you to get to know Tra'var," Damos said.

"No!" She didn't want him to go.

His expression softened. Just a little, but it was enough for her to grasp that something else was going on. Tall, dark, and golden had doubts too? Okay. That made her feel a little better.

"Then I will stay." His lips quirked up into a tiny smile that made her stomach all quivery.

"Good. That's good. Uh. Sit. I'll be right back. I don't know about you, but I could really use a drink before we have this conversation." And during it. And probably several more afterward.

"You do not need to make us something to drink, *mahaya*. I am happy to go downstairs and order us something from your tavern," Tra'var spoke this time.

"If you go back down there, Saral will want to know why you're not here with me, and then the whole place will watch while you get interrogated. You might think you're tough, but believe me, that female will have you spilling your deepest secrets inside a few minutes."

Both of them laughed. "She would take that as a compliment," Damos muttered.

"You know her?"

"She bought several knives from us. Gifts for her *mahoyen* when they started a new job... which I now realize must have been to celebrate their coming to work for you," Damos said, his voice a pleasantly low rumble now.

"Those are yours?" She knew which blades he was talking about. They were identical in almost every aspect save for the color of the handles. They were elegant and oddly beautiful for something so dangerous—as much works of art as practical tools. So these were the craftsmen who'd made them. More information fell into place. "You're the forge masters I've heard some of the others talking about. The ones who made Maggie and Striker's *kes'tarvs*."

Tra'var looked pleased. "We are. They talk about our work?"

"All the time. Maggie was going to take me to your shop someday so I could talk to you about buying a *kes'tarv* for myself." The metal baton could extend into a quarterstaff of sorts, serving as simple practical weapon she could keep behind the bar.

"Do you know how to wield one?" Damos asked.

"Uh. No. Maggie was going to show me."

"We will teach you," Damos declared. "It would be our honor. Though you will not need one now that we know you are our *mahaya*. We will protect you."

Oh no. That wasn't going to work. She did not need to be protected, cosseted or treated like a Tiskalien ice orchid. "That isn't necessary. I've always taken care of myself. We can add that to the list of things we have to talk about. But not until I get drinks. This won't take long."

She shrugged out of the massive coat still draped around her shoulders and handed it back to Damos. Then she slapped her hand on the palm scanner and fled inside the moment the door unlocked.

She needed a moment to think, or at least to try, and that wasn't going to happen when she was standing next to the twin avatars of temptation on her deck.

Three deep breaths later, she had enough clarity of mind to realize she'd bolted like a scalded *peskin*. Feeling foolish, she stuck her head back outside. "Have you eaten yet?"

"No. We had intended to enjoy a meal inside with

Striker and Maggie and the others." Tra'var shrugged. "But then you happened."

"Okay. Two afterburner cocktails and two orders of Almost Heaven coming up." She ducked back inside, ignoring the exclamations of surprise from her two guests. She was not ready to think of them as her mates. Not even close, in fact.

Her food dispenser was programmed with everything on her bar's menu, but she didn't use it. Instead, she tapped out a quick request on her comms and sent it to the kitchen downstairs.

Not five seconds later, she had a response. *"On its way."*

"How the hell does she do that?" Anya muttered aloud and went over to the chute she had added to the tavern's design before they'd even broken ground. It ran from her small eating area to the Bar None's kitchen.

Sure enough, the little mag-lev platform was already on its way up by the time she got the door open. It held a tray with the requested drinks and desserts, along with a liqueur-laced coffee and an appetizer platter generous enough to feed half the guests seated downstairs.

She picked up the tray, turned, and gave an undignified squeak of surprise when she saw both males in the still-open doorway. They hadn't set foot inside her place, but they were as close to the threshold as they could manage without crossing it.

"What are you? Space vampires? Can't you come in without permission?" she asked.

"What is a vampire?" Damos asked.

"A fanged, flying, blood-sucking monster from human folklore that can't enter a victim's house without an invitation. It was a bad joke. Forget I said anything. I've got our drinks, time to—"

"You think I'm a monster?" Damos stepped back and vanished from sight.

"What? No!" She almost dropped the tray as she raced to the door, afraid he'd already left. If he flew off before she could explain...

Tra'var caught her at the door, removed the tray from her hands, and then stepped back to reveal that Damos hadn't left. He stood by the railing of her little patio, his hands gripping the metal with his wings spread.

"I'm sorry. I was babbling because I was nervous. That's all. I know you're not monsters. You're Vardarians, and my guests." She cautiously walked over and stood beside Damos. When he didn't move, she reached out and placed her hand on his. "Can we try that again?"

They stood in silence long enough Anya decided her overture had been rejected. It wasn't until she moved away that he reacted. He turned his hand over and captured her fingers with his.

That's when she noticed his talons.

"You're wrong. Tra'var is Vardarian. Most beings believe *I* am a monster."

There was no missing the darkness in his voice or the hard jut of his jaw as he spoke.

She kept her hand in his and turned to face him. He was so tall she had to tip her head back so she could meet his amber gaze. "Most beings are *fraxxing* idiots. I don't know much about you yet, but I already know that whoever you are, you're not a monster."

He hadn't meant to say it like that. He hadn't intended to say it at all. Not yet. But he had and now...

Anya smiled up at him, her eyes a fascinating blend of green and golden brown. Her pheromones swirled around the enclosed space, enticing and enchanting him. She was lovely with a kind smile that deepened the lines at the corners of her mouth. But that kindness was tempered with strength.

"It pleases me that you think so." He touched her cheek with his free hand, careful to keep his talons away from her soft skin.

She narrowed her eyes, the corners of her mouth folding downward. "It doesn't please me to know you think of yourself that way." She deliberately raised her hand to cover his, pressing it to her cheek. "I don't know about you, but I came here to get away from other beings' opinions."

He waited for her to ask about his talons or why he considered himself something other than Vardarian.

She didn't. She just stood there quietly and waited.

Tra'var was loud enough for both of them. He threw back his head and laughed long and hard. "It seems our ancestors picked well, my brother."

To his shock, Anya turned her head and fixed Tra'var with a stare that a sand *vipa* would envy. "You knew he felt this way and haven't helped him to work through it? I thought *anrik* were closer than brothers?"

Tra'v stopped mid-chuckle and raised his arm to show her the scar on his wrist. "We are. Which is why I am delighted to have an ally to help me change his ways. Damos can be as difficult as a *gharshtu* with a headache."

"I see. So I'm getting a fixer-upper package."

He wasn't sure what that meant, and neither was his translator. "What did you call us?" Damos asked.

Tra'var moved closer, corralling her between them without quite making contact. "I think she said we are what the humans call a work in progress."

Damos broke the tension with a joke. "That's accurate enough. Tra'var would starve if not for me and our technology. He has almost no ability to prepare food on his own. Even the food dispenser has been confounded by some of his requests." He lowered his voice. "Do not agree to try his *nagari*. He's convinced it's edible. I am not."

"Don't listen to him. He's still alive. Isn't he? Thus, it's edible. In fact, it's delicious," Tra'var protested.

It was an exaggeration. Tra'var had improved as a cook over the years, but the banter was safe and did what Damos hoped, making Anya relax. He wanted her to enjoy these moments. As unsettled as he was by the idea that they'd somehow gained a mate, he knew better than to fight this. The *sharhal* was all-consuming. Trying to resist would only damage their new relationship... and change nothing.

He also knew that in time, she'd change her mind about him. She would realize he was a monster. When that happened, she'd withdraw from him and spend her time with his *anrik*. It was inevitable. He'd always known that would be the way it went, though maybe with a human female it would take longer. After all, she didn't have the same biases as a Vardarian female.

Forge and flames, he hoped so.

Her touch calmed him enough that his talons retracted and his scales relaxed. That had never happened before, but this was his *mahaya*. Her pheromones perfumed the air with a heady scent. If she asked him to fly to the stars and bring her back one to wear in her hair, he'd do it. He was losing his *qarfing* mind.

"Fortunately, I happen to have three of the best chefs on the planet working for me. Once I find out what *nagari* is, I'll have Saral make it and then we can do a taste test," Anya said with a laugh.

"It's noodles with a simple cheese sauce," Tra'var explained.

"Noodles with..." Anya burst out laughing. "I didn't know Vardarians had a version of mac and cheese! Even I can make that. We are definitely having a taste test one of these days. Maybe for once I won't come in last."

"You can't cook?" Tra'var looked puzzled. "But you own a tavern."

"I know my strengths. I can run a bar and mix a mean cocktail, but cooking isn't something I ever learned."

"Your mother never taught you?" Tra'var asked.

Anya laughed even louder. "My mother? *Fraxx* no. She taught me how to count cards and shoot straight. She doesn't cook. Ever."

"She sounds formidable," Damos said. Most of the Vardarian females he'd met held a different kind of power. They were rarer than males and used that to their advantage any way they could.

"That's a polite word for it. When she gets back, she's going to want to meet you both. If she doesn't scare you off, maybe there's hope for us." Anya clamped her lips together, her eyes wide. She clearly hadn't intended on saying that last bit out loud.

"Nothing is going to scare us off, Anya. That is not how this works." Tra'var set a gentle hand on their *mahaya's* neck, brushing his thumb over the side of her throat. "You are ours, and we are yours. Forever. I know that is not the human way, but so far, every match between our races has plotted the same course. We will be together for the rest of our lives."

"You don't know that. You can't. There haven't been that many matches yet. What if we're not really compatible? I mean, I know about the Reekar. Some of your species have gone into the *sharhal* with one of them but the bond doesn't last. Right?"

Damos fought the urge to snarl. Had he been wrong? Was she already looking for a way to escape?

Tra'var must have sensed his unease because he hurried to explain. "That bond doesn't always last. It also doesn't produce children. With every other species, the matings are permanent."

"And... children?" Anya's voice was suddenly softer.

"Yes," Tra'var said quickly.

Anya shook her head. "Just like that? Boom. Forever and a family. It can't be that easy."

Damos sensed this conversation was in danger of falling out of orbit and making a messy crater on impact. He didn't know what the issue was. Too many were in play at the moment to even guess. "Is this too much? Too soon?"

Tra'var shot him a surprised look. "Too soon?"

"Yes. It's too... everything," Anya agreed. "So, how about we sit down and talk for a while? Get to know each other. Unless..." She sighed. "How long do we have?"

"Long enough," Tra'var said. "We're young enough that the *sharhal* will take time to reach full strength. A day or so, maybe."

"A day?" Anya repeated, her voice rising half an octave. She blew out a breath that held a note of sharp laughter. "Okay. I can work with that. This might be the shortest courtship in history, but it's something."

"Courtship?" Damos asked. His translator had a definition of the word, but he suspected it meant something different in the human lexicon.

Anya smiled. "The time when a couple, or trio, or whatever, learn about each other and decide if they want to be together permanently. Usually, it involves trying to impress their potential mate with whatever skills they have to offer. In this case, I think we can skip that part."

"No." Tra'var's voice was firm.

She turned her head to look back at him. "No?"

"No. We will not be skipping that part. I'm looking forward to showing you what Damos and I are good at." He grinned, and Damos caught on to his meaning.

"I think we should start with a demonstration of how well we work together," he said. He drew her into his arms as Tra'var moved in closer behind her. This time they didn't keep their distance. They pressed up against her, sandwiching her soft body between them. Tra'var dipped his head to nibble on her earlobe as Damos allowed himself to lean down and brush a barely there kiss to Anya's lovely mouth.

"Oh..." Anya breathed, and then her arms were around his neck as she rose on her toes to kiss him back with an eagerness that nearly shattered his control.

No female had ever kissed him so willingly. It was... he stopped trying to search for the words and focused on Anya. The warmth of her lips. The scent of her arousal and need. She fit perfectly between them, and something was achingly intimate about sharing her this way with Tra'var.

In time, Tra'var turned her toward him, claiming their mate's mouth with a tender hunger that echoed his own. She was just as eager with his *anrik* as she had been with him, and it was surprisingly arousing to watch them together. His hands still lingered on her body, the scent of her wrapping around him like an invisible caress.

They'd never done this. Not once in all their years together. But this was different. This was Anya. Their shining star. Their *mahaya*.

3

———

Two hours later, Anya watched the pair descend the stairs and disappear into the snow-filled night.

She hadn't wanted them to go, but she also needed some time alone. Her lips still tingled from their last kiss good night as first Tra'var and then Damos had taken her into their arms and kissed her until her knees threatened to buckle. She felt like the gravity had been reduced by half and almost floated back inside her apartment, feeling as giddy as a girl coming home from her first date.

It was equally enjoyable and frustrating. She'd never felt this good, but it was affecting her ability to think clearly. Now they were gone, she really needed some time to process the evening's events.

It was time to break out the big guns. She raided her private stash at the back of her cooler and poured herself a large glass of *jazza* berry juice. It was her childhood favorite, and her mom kept her well-stocked with the real thing, made from berries from the Pheran home world.

She sank down into her favorite chair, sighed, and then raised her glass in a solitary toast. "Farewell, single life. Apparently, I'm a sort-of-maybe married woman now."

After a few more sips she closed her eyes and tried to sort through the whirling thoughts filling her head. It was impossible. Every time she tried to focus, memories of the kisses they'd shared would crowd out everything else.

Fraxx it. She was going to need help to work through this, and she only trusted one being to give her some much-needed information about Vardarian mating rites. She needed to talk to Saral. She sent a quick text message to her head chef, asking how things were going downstairs.

The reply was almost instantaneous, and it wasn't a text message. Saral sent a vid-connect request.

Anya laughed and accepted the call.

"Why are you alone?" Saral demanded, her frowning face filling the screen.

"Because they went home."

Saral's brow furrowed deeper. "Why? What happened? That is... but why?" It was rare for the Vardarian female to be at a loss for words.

"Because we all agreed that's what was best."

Saral snorted. "Best for who? No, don't answer

that. I'll be right up. Antas can finish up without me. This is an emergency!"

"It's really not," Anya tried to protest but stopped when she realized Saral had disconnected. She was talking to herself.

Not even a minute later she heard the telltale thump of a Vardarian setting down on her patio followed by a second, heavier one. Saral hadn't come alone.

She reached the door and opened it without waiting for them to announce themselves. "Did you fly straight over the tavern?" she asked.

Saral nodded. "Fastest way. Straight up. Straight down. Are you alright?"

"I'm fine. I mean. Mostly. Considering I just discovered I'm mated to a pair of strangers and my entire life has been turned upside down by a random act of biology."

N'tev appeared behind his mate. "It is so much more than that."

"But I understand why you are feeling uncertain," Saral interjected, cutting off what Anya suspected was the beginning of a lecture she didn't want to hear right now.

N'tev was the somber one of their trio, the stalwart rock that his mate and *anrik* relied on to keep the trio stable. While she appreciated his advice, it wasn't helpful right now. First, she needed a little more time to panic.

Saral came in and immediately caught Anya up in a hug. "What do you need from us?"

Anya hugged her friend back. "This is a good start. I'm just... mates? Me? I never imagined. Not to mention the fact that with my track record, if there is a way to screw this up, I'll find it. Your kind don't do divorce, though. Right? So when this goes sideways, then what?"

"It will not go sideways," Saral said with utter conviction.

"I wouldn't make any bets on that. I mean, you've met my mother. Shipwreck relationships are a family specialty. Generations of bad judgment are working against me here."

N'tev stepped inside, and the door closed behind him. "That isn't an issue here. This is the will of the ancestors. I struggle to understand how you humans choose your mates." He shrugged. "From what I have learned, you don't seem very good at it."

"Some are. Some aren't. I am definitely in the latter category."

"Then perhaps you should see this as a boon." Saral guided both Anya and her mate into the sitting area, and they all took a seat.

"You mean not having a choice is a good thing?" Anya asked.

"If you doubt your own judgment so much, then yes. I think it might be. My people have never chosen our mates. For me, the day I met N'tev and Antas was the happiest of my life. Not every mating is perfect, but it's exceptionally rare for a trio to be unhappy unless one or more parties makes a deliberate choice to be contrary."

"Like Kade's parents," Anya said. She'd met the male's fathers at his bonding ceremony to Shadow and Denz. Kade's mother had not attended, and while the older Vardarian males had chosen to move to the colony and build a new shipyard in orbit around Liberty, so far, no one had heard or seen anything more from Kade's mother. Being trapped in a relationship with incompatible partners forever was a fate she wanted to avoid.

"Yes. As I understand it, Evita created a rift between herself and her *mahoyen* because she resents their affection for each other. That is still a bias some members of the higher classes hold on to." Saral shot her mate a wicked glance. "It is their loss. There is nothing more arousing than the sight of my beloved pleasuring each other."

Anya had to take a drink to avoid making eye contact with either of them for a few seconds. Saral's blunt honesty about her love life was refreshing, but occasionally it made for awkward moments like this. It was one of the many cultural differences she'd noticed between the three main races that made up the colony, though the cyborgs had no concept of modesty and were almost as sexually open as the Vardarians.

Almost.

Once she'd regained her composure, Anya spoke

again, ignoring the merry twinkle in Saral's eyes. "So these matings can fail."

"If one or more of the parties work to make it unpleasant, yes. But that's an unusual choice for someone to make. It takes a great deal of energy to resist the links that bind us, and the bond doesn't fade quickly. It's a slow, painful experience for everyone involved." N'tev reached out and took Saral's hand. "We still fight, of course. But as my beloved will tell you, that leads to some of the most pleasurable hours of sex we have ever experienced."

"Now you're both doing it." A thought struck her. "Oh no. Who made the bet about making me blush and how much did you just win?" Anya was well aware of her employees' love of making impromptu bets with each other and some of their regular customers.

"I believe Striker now owes his mate several orgasms. He also has to take my son and his *anrik* for several training sessions with his new team of rangers."

N'tev looked startled. "He does?"

"He does." Saral beamed. "It's time they spread their wings somewhere a little farther away from home. *Much* farther."

"They are old enough," N'tev agreed, nodding.

"You volunteered them for the ranger program?" Anya stared at Saral. "Aren't they going to be unhappy about that?"

"If they don't like my idea, they are welcome to come up with another one. Neither of them has chosen a profession yet. They had aspirations of playing professional *balti*, but that sport requires wealth and influence far beyond our means. They had hoped to be picked up by one of the smaller teams but..."

N'tev shook his head. "It was not to be. They chose to come to Haven with us."

Anya smiled. "I see. They've been enjoying an extended vacation and you think it's time it ended."

"Yes," Saral said and then twitched a finger at Anya. "But that is a different subject than the one we came here to discuss. If you have questions, ask them."

She had dozens of questions. No, more like hundreds of them, if not thousands. Most of them she'd have to ask Tra'var and Damos in person, but she needed to know some things *now*.

"What do you know about them? Tra'v and Damos, I mean." She hadn't meant to shorten Tra'var's name, but that's how she thought of him. *Great.* Her brain was assigning nicknames already.

"They are hardworking and skilled masters of their craft," N'tev said.

Saral gave her mate a sideways look of amusement. "Is that what you said about me? I think Anya is looking for some less practical information."

N'tev smiled. "I said you were the most beautiful female I had ever seen. At least, that's all I remember now."

"Mhmm. We'll discuss your memory of events another time. Perhaps Antas can help fill in the gaps."

"The only gaps I'm interested in filling are..." N'tev

broke off when Saral raised a brow at him. "Right. Anya first. Gaps later."

"Is this what I have to look forward to?" Anya asked, waving her hand at N'tev.

"I hope so," Saral said.

So did she, and Anya couldn't tell if it was her head, her heart, or the *sharhal* making the call.

"As to your question. They are not overly social, but from what I've heard they are well-liked and respected. A few are uneasy about Damos, but that's understandable given his differences."

"Differences?" Anya raised one hand and wiggled her fingers. "Like the retractable talons?" She wanted to ask if that was why he'd referred to himself as a monster, but that had been a private confession just between the three of them.

"And his wings," N'tev confirmed. "He's the only one who trains exclusively on the ground. He cannot fly well, or for long."

"Was he injured? I thought your people had nanotech to fix things like that."

"Not injured, no. It's the way he was born. At least, that's what I've heard. His mother was not a pure Vardarian. She must have been overlooked for the usual tests and in-utero adjustments." Saral said it so casually it took Anya a moment to grasp what she was really saying.

"What adjustments?" she prompted.

"To ensure that all children are a physical match to their Vardarian parents. It is optional, of course, but if it's not done, the child will face a certain amount of... let's call it resistance in society. Especially in the heart of the empire."

Anya wanted to rail and rant in horror, but she couldn't. Humans were hardly in a position to judge other races. They had their own biases and failures to overcome. But what Saral was talking about sounded alarmingly like genetic purification, and the idea blew a very large hole in the hull of the theory that the Vardarians were the superior race. Not that they ever made that claim, but she and many of the others had assumed it.

Apparently they were wrong.

"So Damos isn't pure Vardarian? He looks like one."

"He is not. Given his appearance and the talons, I'd assume he is part Ferrym. They're one of the few races in the galaxy we can procreate with. In fact, a link in our genomes indicates we share a common ancestor, though no one is sure how we ended up inhabiting different planetary systems with no awareness of each other until a few hundred years ago," Saral said.

"I had no idea," Anya said.

"It's another reason colonies like this one are created from time to time. Not everyone agrees with the practice, or the bias against those who didn't undergo the procedures. I imagine that's one of the reasons why Damos and his *anrik* are here."

That made sense. Just about everyone here was

looking for a chance to reset their lives one way or another.

N'tev leaned forward, his voice pitched low. "If you are concerned about it, of course you can still have the procedure done on your own children. They could be pure Vardarian and no one would question your choice."

"My children?" Great googly galaxies. She hadn't even considered that. Humans lived well over a hundred years these days, but women still only had a limited supply of eggs. She was over forty, which meant the odds of her having children now was... Damn. She had no idea. But kids hadn't been a consideration for her in a very long time.

"There's no reason you couldn't have their children. They are a source of great joy. Also, frustration, sleeplessness, and fury, but mostly joy." Saral smiled.

"Sounds like the job I have now, only I get to sleep in every morning," Anya joked.

"After running bars all these years, I think you'll find parenting remarkably easy," Saral said.

"And alarmingly similar," N'tev agreed.

They talked a while longer, answering questions about how the *sharhal* would likely progress and what she should expect. It helped to know the details, and it was much easier to think while she was away from her potential mates. Now she understood why that was—pheromones. She wasn't aware of them, but her body reacted to them anyway. The longer she was in their company, the stronger the effect.

She returned to the tavern with N'tev and Saral. The snow hadn't stopped yet, and she took a few minutes to play in it before the cold drove her inside. The place was already empty, and it didn't take long to cash out and close up for the night. The whole time, her head was full of thoughts of Damos, Tra'var, and what her future might look like now.

She'd only signed a three-year contract for this place. Unlike the rest of Haven's citizens, she had no nanotech and didn't plan to get it any time soon. It meant she was free to leave at any time. She'd wanted that. Hell, she'd insisted on having that choice.

And now she didn't have it anymore. At least, not unless she found a way to break the mating bond already forming between her and her alien mates.

Tra'var didn't need his wings tonight. He was flying high on the knowledge that they had found their *mahaya*. She wasn't what he'd envisioned, but that didn't matter. She was theirs.

When they reached their home in the artist's quarter, he ignored the front door and went to the side gate instead. He was too excited to sleep and had a hundred different ideas in his head about things they'd need to make for Anya. A dagger, for one thing. And jewelry with gemstones to match her eyes.

Damos followed him, catching hold of his wrist as he headed to the forge.

"Where the *qarf* are you going?"

"To get started. We have a lot of work to do. What sort of blade do you think she'd like? I'm thinking something elegant. Maybe *tarchozin* with some gold inlaid in the hilt—"

"Stop," Damos said, and something in his tone made Tra'var pause and turn to look at him.

"What is it?"

"We can't do this yet." Damos was being cryptic, which usually meant he wasn't happy but didn't know how to express himself.

"Yet? Oh, right! It's late. The neighbors won't appreciate it if we fire up the forge and start banging on metal. We can start first thing in the morning."

Damos' jaw tightened. "No." The word came out through gritted teeth.

"No what? I'm going to need some more words. I'm a little distracted at the moment." He slapped Damos' arm. "We found her!"

"We did. But she's not Vardarian."

"And? Don't tell me that's going to be an issue for you."

"Don't." Damos snarled at him.

Tra'var heard the warning in it. He just wasn't sure what the warning was about. "Don't what? I have no idea what you're trying to tell me and getting snarly isn't going to help."

"Don't accuse me of being biased. You know that's not it."

"I didn't!" Tra'var pointed back to the house. "But clearly we need to have this conversation inside."

Damos turned on his heel and stomped inside. One look at his back and Tra'var knew how unhappy his *anrik* was. His wings were out again, which meant his scales were raised. Was this something to do with the *sharhal's* affect? The Ferrym were more aggressive than Vardarians. Maybe this was normal for them. He'd need to do some reading tonight. But only once the two of them had talked.

The back door led into their storage room. It was full of raw materials, partially finished projects, racks of weapons and cases full of jewelry waiting its turn to be displayed in the main store that took up the rest of the first floor.

They lived above the shop, though that might need to change now they'd found Anya. She'd need space of her own, and with the redesign, this residence only had two bedrooms.

Damos rounded on him the moment the door was shut. "Never accuse me of being biased against another being because of their species again."

His skin was bright gold, and a quick glance at his hands told Tra'var that his *anrik* was agitated enough his talons had reappeared.

"I wasn't sure what you meant, but I apologize. I should have worded it differently."

"Yes. You should have."

The words were bitten off so short Tra'var could almost see the teeth marks. "My head isn't clear, and neither is yours. I am sorry, but I still don't understand why you're so angry. This is it, my brother. We have our *mahaya!*"

"That's the problem right there." Damos picked up an unfinished blade from a work table and twirled it between his fingers as he spoke. "We don't have her yet. You need to slow down. If this is going to work, you can't proceed the way we would if Anya were Vardarian."

"Why? Her desire for us was as clear as the air above us. How can you doubt it after the way she kissed us and welcomed us into her home?"

"We didn't enter her home," Damos reminded him.

"But we did kiss her. I didn't imagine that." Tra'var still didn't understand his *anrik's* point. He was unhappy, that much was clear, but the reason for it wasn't.

Damos growled and shoved a hand through his hair, leaving it standing up in unruly spikes. "Desire is not the issue. But we were raised knowing what the *sharhal* was and what it meant. Humans only met our kind for the first time a year or so ago. That means that whatever Anya's understanding of our species is, it's new and likely has gaps big enough to fly a cruiser through."

"But this is our dream. A mate. A family. The three of us complete and happy. A mate to wake up with each morning."

"In whose bed? In whose home? Our mate has her own dreams. She runs a successful business and likes to be close to it for the same reasons we do. Before you start talking about offspring and waking up together, you need to find out what she wants. What I want. We've never discussed offspring and now you're ready to move her in, slap a *harani* on her arm, and name our firstborn before the night is over."

"You don't want children?" Tra'var had assumed Damos would. He had infinite patience with the young ones who sometimes came to watch them work at the forge. The children who had come to Haven with their parents were intrigued by their craft and would pepper them with questions if given half a chance.

"Want is not the issue." He pointed to his wings and then flexed his hands to show off his claws. "But what female would want a child with their father's flaws?"

Now he understood. "One who has already declared that she doesn't think you're a monster." He grinned at Damos. "You're aware you're making the same mistake you just accused me of making. You're right. We haven't spoken to Anya about any of this yet." He extended his arm, hand fisted, the round scar of their blood bonding ritual facing Damos.

Without a word, Damos raised his arm to cross wrists with him, touching their scars together. Then he sighed. Within a few seconds, his talons retracted and his skin lost some of its luster.

"This is..." He tapped a finger to the center of his forehead. "It's hard to think right now."

"And the *sharhal* has only begun. How does anyone resist this for long?" He'd heard the stories of what happened to those who tried to deny the mating fever. They went mad. Many died. He'd known the facts, but now he was experiencing it for himself. Damos was right. He needed to slow down. Beginnings were delicate, and this was an important time for all of them.

"I have no idea, but you need to find a way."

"So what you're saying is... as difficult as it is to be rational right now, I'm going to have to resist the urge to go back to Anya's place and bang on her door until she lets us in so we can claim her tonight?" Tra'var asked. He was mostly joking. Mostly.

Damos snorted. "Don't even think about it."

"Too late for that."

This time, Damos just shook his head. "You are hopeless. Why did I ever agree to be your *anrik?*"

"Because you needed someone who could put up with your broody, grumpy self, and you loved the idea of spending your life playing with fire."

"Ah, right. I knew there was a reason." Damos was smiling now. "And I don't suppose it would hurt to track down that partially finished *tarchozin* blade tonight. It would make a fine dagger for our *mahaya.*"

"I'm glad you agree." They started rummaging through the stacks of materials, both of them setting aside anything they thought might inspire them. It wasn't often that they fought like this, but when they did, it was always about something important.

Anya was the most important thing ever to happen to them. Tra'var had no doubt they were going to fight again.

She'd be worth it.

4

———

ANYA WASN'T A MORNING PERSON. Her mother often teased that the last time Anya had been awake at the crack of dawn was the day she was born.

It was probably true.

By the time she was out of bed and ready to face the day, the rest of the colony had usually been active for at least a few hours. Today felt different. The usual day sounds were muffled and some of them were unfamiliar. Scraping and banging noises drew her to the nearest window out of curiosity.

The sky was covered with a thick layer of lead-gray cloud and the ground was thick with snow. The change was startling. What little sunlight made it through the clouds reflected off the snow in new ways.

Any other day, she would have camped out by the window with her mug of tea to watch. It was fascinating to see her neighbors use everything from push brooms and broad-headed shovels to some sort of tech she'd never seen before to clear the snow from their doors and market stalls. Today wasn't a normal day, though. Not even close.

Today she'd be spending time getting to know her *mahoyen* and trying to reconcile her need to always have an exit plan with the reality she was now faced with. Damos and Tra'var were her destined mates, and unless she deliberately sabotaged their trio, she would be with them forever.

Forever.

Just the word made her want to pack a bag and flee back to outer space. She didn't do long-term relationships. *Veth*, she didn't do long-term anything. Even her contract for the Bar None had a shorter renewal time than the norm. Commitment wasn't a concept she was comfortable with. She should have known the universe would see that as a challenge. Now she was matched with two males whose biology was hard-wired for everything she wasn't.

A surge of annoyance hit and she looked skyward, both hands raised in an obscene gesture. "*Fraxx* you, universe."

It was a pointless, petty little rebellion that would probably earn her even more unpleasantness in the future, but she didn't care. She'd been away from her living, breathing temptations long enough the *sharhal* was barely a whisper in her blood right now. That meant she was thinking clearly and free to lash out at whatever force had made this happen.

The logical part of her mind knew this clarity was only temporary, but the rest of her was trying to convince herself that last night was all a mistake and she wasn't really fated to spend forever with Tra'var and Damos.

Anya didn't believe in destiny. Sometimes things worked out and sometimes they didn't. It wasn't fate or luck. It was all just hard work, perseverance, and random acts of chaos. And in her particular case, a genetic anomaly led to the women of her family to make catastrophically bad relationship choices. Or maybe they were cursed. Her mother believed it was the latter. Anya wasn't sure. It was hard to justify believing in curses when she refused to believe in fate or luck, but some days it was hard to deny the possibility.

She checked her messages while she drank her tea and waited for all her brain cells to make the transition to wakefulness. She had several notes from the local business group she belonged to discussing the weather and what it meant for business as well as two from Saral with extra tidbits of information and links to information on Vardarian mating rituals in the colony's database.

The link led to a whole section about it. Clearly she wasn't the only one who had questions.

She also had a vid message from her mom with a

status update that included info on where she was off to next. Anya was relieved to hear that Hezza had added a few more stops to her itinerary and wouldn't be back on Liberty until next month. That meant Anya had time to come to terms with her change in status before her mother returned to cause her own special brand of havoc.

She saved the best for last—a vid message from Tra'var and Damos time stamped several hours ago. *Veth.* Were they morning beings? The universe wasn't that cruel. Was it?

Their handsome faces both appeared on the screen and she did her best to ignore the flutter deep in her belly. Just the sight of them made her pulse race as heat that had nothing to do with her tea flooded her body.

"Hello, Anya. If you are agreeable, we would like to escort you to our home today and show you around our shop. In fact, we'd like to spend the day with you, at least until you need to attend to your own business." Tra'var smiled. "I promise there will be food, too, and Damos has insisted I don't try to cook you anything."

"You are never cooking for her. Or me," Damos grumbled.

Anya laughed and touched their faces on the screen. She really had it bad. Watching two men bicker and grumble should not be sexy, but it was.

She watched the rest of the message and went to hit reply but then remembered she hadn't done more than make tea yet this morning.

"Computer, reflective surface please."

The wall nearest her shimmered and shifted to mirror mode. One look and she knew she'd been right to check. Some of her hair had escaped its braid while she slept and was stuck out from her head at odd angles. She had a crease mark in one cheek from her pillow, and the hours she'd spent tossing and turning showed clearly in the shadows under her eyes. If she really wanted a way out of this relationship, all she had to do was let them see her looking like this.

She decided to text back instead. She had some time today. She could do any office work before it got busy and N'tev had promised to deal with the snow removal, so she had no reason to decline their invitation.

She arranged to meet them downstairs in an hour. Then she hurried to her sanitation cubby, her hands already busy unbraiding the rest of her hair.

Maybe today she'd leave it loose.

She was waiting on the front porch of the Bar None five minutes before they were due to arrive. Thanks to the winter weather, she was wearing her warmest boots and a heavy cloak with a hood. It wasn't a fashion she was familiar with, but given how warm and comfortable it was, she suspected she'd be adopting it as her regular outerwear for the rest of the winter. As an added bonus, her unbound hair was tucked beneath the fabric and wouldn't blow around in the wind.

To her amusement, her entire kitchen staff had shown up early today. Antas claimed he needed extra time to prep today's menu. N'tev was busy clearing away the last traces of ice and snow from around the bar. He'd even brought his son and his *anrik*, B'ron and Kotar. The younger Vardarians had been told to make themselves useful and were currently helping to clear a walkway down the middle of the bridge.

"Are you going to tell them that the bridge was engineered so that it could clear itself of snow?" she asked Saral. The female wasn't even trying to look busy. She leaned against the wall and watched Anya try not to fidget as she waited for her dates to arrive.

"No. The energy of youth is infinite. Better they use it for the good of the community and save the power for other things, like heat." Saral held out a hand. Her fingers were trembling. "I cannot seem to get warm today."

"Then why are you out here? Inside. Go! Make yourself a cup of cocoa or something and supervise Antas instead of me."

"You're no fun."

"Fun has nothing to do with it. If you get sick, who is going to run the bar when this whole *sharhal* thing kicks into high gear?"

"So, you've accepted that will happen?" Saral looked pleased.

"Mostly. I am aware that wishful thinking will never win out against science."

"Or destiny," Saral added.

"I'm not ready to have that conversation. You. Inside. Now."

"Bossy. You do realize that Vardarians don't get sick. We have nanotech that prevents it."

"I'm bossy because that's my job description. As in, I am your boss. Now, shoo! Even if you can't get sick, there's no sense in you sitting out here shivering."

Saral threw up her hands and laughed. "I'm going. I'm going. You'll make a good mother someday, my friend. You already have the right tone."

Anya ignored the comment. She had enough on her mind without considering the added complication of potential motherhood. It had never been part of her plans. It was probably too late for her anyway, and at some point, she was going to have to tell Tra'v and Damos about that. Their species lived so much longer than humans, she had no idea if they'd even realized it was a potential issue.

Fraxx. She had no idea how old they were! What if she was robbing the cradle? Anxious thoughts and worries exploded in her mind like a swarm of micro-meteors. They zipped around, colliding and connecting with each other, every contact adding to the mayhem until she was almost overwhelmed with doubt.

She was saved by their arrival a few minutes later. Her worries vanished in a heartbeat, swept away by a flash flood of desire as the *sharhal* rekindled.

She recognized them immediately, despite the fact they were little more than dark figures against the snow. It was something in the way they moved, or maybe a trace of their pheromones on the winter wind. She hadn't intended to, but she found herself stepping out to meet them.

They wore the same long jackets as yesterday, but today their hoods were up to keep out the cold. It didn't matter, though. She could still tell them apart. Tra'var was slightly taller while Damos was broader.

Once they saw her, they both sped up, their hands raised in greeting.

Around her, all activity stopped. The bridge and everyone on it watched with blatant curiosity as the three of them reunited. When Tra'var swept her into his arms, they all cheered.

She blushed and cursed under her breath. "Saral has a big mouth,"

Then all her attention was on the two males crowded around her. "Hi."

Tra'var didn't say a word. He just crushed his mouth to hers. She'd thought last night's kisses had been hot, but this was... holy *fraxx*. She was surprised the surrounding snow didn't spontaneously melt away. He locked one arm around her waist and hauled her up against him, his other hand buried in her hair. His lips were warm and their breath mingled in a cloud of vapor as she opened her mouth with a soft sound of pleasure she barely recognized as her own.

Heat and need rushed through her veins like the purest pharma in the galaxy, elevating her senses and filling her with a hunger that nothing would ease—nothing but more of this from both of them.

She rose on her toes, fingers tangled in both their coats to pull herself higher. Strong hands gripped her hips, and a second later she was off the ground as Tra'var picked her up.

Damos—at least she thought it was Damos—wrapped an arm under her ass to steady her. "I've got you."

The cheering got louder. She ignored it.

Tra'var chuckled, the low sound rising from his throat and rolling through her body at the same time. "It seems we have an audience again."

"They can look all they want. Only *we* may touch," Damos declared. His words were a whisper against her ear.

She turned her head to kiss him, one hand still curled in each of their coats. "That goes for all the females, too. Any unauthorized touching and someone gets shot."

Damos growled and captured her lips with his. His kiss was pure possession, demanding and forceful. She gasped and he took advantage, his tongue slipping into her mouth to tangle with hers.

"I think what he's trying to say is there will be no one else for us. Not ever," Tra'var said, his voice thick with desire and more than a little laughter.

"Yes. That." Damos broke the kiss to stare into her eyes, the amber depths almost glowing with the heat of his passion. "I thought my meaning was clear."

"Oh it was," she assured him. "But maybe you should tell me again just so I'm sure I understood."

"With pleasure." Damos kissed her again, hot and hungry, while Tra'var slid a hand between her body and his to cup her breast in one large hand. Even through her cloak, she could still feel the warmth of his touch.

"Too many clothes," he muttered. "Why did we have to find you on the eve of winter?"

He sounded so frustrated it made her laugh again, the sound captured by Damos' mouth.

If this was what it would be like to be mated to this pair, maybe it wouldn't be so bad.

Damos hadn't slept. His mind was spinning faster than a wind turbine in a maelstrom, and he kept rising from his bed to prowl around the house and yard. Tra'var claimed he hadn't slept much either, but Damos had heard the snores coming from his *anrik's* room and knew he'd gotten at least some rest.

It concerned him that he was reacting differently to the *sharhal*. He shouldn't be. One of the reasons for the blood bonding ritual was to ensure that both males were in sync when it came to choosing a mate. He'd often worried that his flawed genetics would interfere with the *sharhal*, but he'd always assumed Tra'var would have the stronger reaction.

He never imagined it would be him.

Her laughter held notes of desire that had him hard and aching. He could feel his scales tightening, though it wasn't enough to trigger any other changes. He growled her name and nipped her lower lip without thinking. Then he broke the kiss to apologize.

At least, that was the plan. Anya had something else in mind.

She moaned and chased his mouth, kissing him again before letting her teeth sink into his lip for one brief moment. It was enough to send most of the blood in his body rushing to his cock. His knees nearly buckled, the urge to drop to the snow and cover her with his body so powerful he almost gave in to it.

Fortunately Tra'var still had hold of Anya, too, saving her from a chilly encounter with the bridge.

"That is..." Tra'var paused to swallow hard. "You are the most enticing creature, Anya. But there are things we need to explain. Biting is, uh, potentially risky."

Damos wanted to smack his *anrik* and tell him to shut up. If she bit him and drew blood, it would just speed up the process. Right now, that's exactly what he wanted.

Only, it shouldn't be. He reined in the primal, possessive thoughts and blew out a sharp breath. His gaze met Tra'var's and the two shared a look that communicated his *anrik* knew what had almost happened.

"Biting is bad?" she asked softly.

Forge and flame. Was that disappointment he

heard in her voice? Because if it was... "No. Well, yes. But also no. Biting is good. Very good. But if you draw blood and taste it? That will just accelerate the *sharhal*."

"Ah. So, biting good, but not until we've gotten to know each other better." She nodded. "I thought that only worked one way. You bite me and that's it, we're mated."

"That too," Tra'var said. He was grinning like a fool now. A smitten one. "But after that, feel free to bite us anytime you like, *mahaya*."

Now he had control again, Damos was painfully aware of the attention they'd attracted. He hated being noticed. "I think it's time we left."

"Yes," Anya agreed and then raised her voice. "Because if we stay any longer no one on this bridge is going to get any work done today."

With a round of chuckles, most of their onlookers went back to their tasks. He and Tra'var carefully set Anya on her feet and turned back the way they'd come.

Damos had intended for them to walk back single file, with Anya in the middle so they could protect her. Not that there was anything to protect her from in the middle of the colony, but the instinct was too strong to ignore.

She changed the plan by reaching out to both of them and taking their hands. "Is your forge fired up? By the time we get there, I suspect I'm going to want to huddle near it for a bit of warmth. I'm used to the nicely regulated air temperature of ships and stations."

Tra'var winked at her. "You do not need the forge. If you are chilled, Damos and I are happy to warm you."

She was silent for a moment and then laughed. "I'll let you know, my *mahoyen*."

Tra'var's voice was in his head a second later. "*You see? She already claims us openly. There's no need to worry, my brother. This is proceeding quickly.*"

"*Do not rush her,*" Damos sent back. Tra'var was as headstrong as he was, but he was also an optimist. He believed the world could be made better by sheer will. Damos knew better.

They chatted the whole walk to their home. Inconsequential topics, mostly. The weather, their chosen professions, and eventually they discussed her plans to approach the council. She wanted them to consider developing the bridge into a market district that spanned the river and extended onto the banks on either side.

"We're going to need another bridge soon, anyway —one that is wide and strong enough to support vehicles," she said.

Tra'var frowned. "Why? There's not much on that side of the river except the barracks the cyborgs used to live in. Only a few human colonists are living there at the moment, and they'll be moving to our side of the river once they're finished the integration training."

"That's why," Anya said.

"What is?" Damos asked, confused.

"Tra'v said *our* side of the river, which suggests the

river divides the colony into two different camps. That goes against the whole concept of Haven. There is just one colony, which is why a group of us deliberately choose to establish businesses in the middle of the bridge. Phaedra helped us sell the idea to the council once. I hope she can do it again now it's time to expand on the concept."

"You want to create a town center, only in the middle of the river." Damos understood now.

"Exactly. Next spring more colonists will be coming here from both Earth and the Vardarian Empire. Haven will grow quickly, and the next development needs to happen on the *other* side of the river."

"To keep things balanced." Tra'var nodded. "With the market in the middle."

She smiled mischievously. "And all those hungry, thirsty folks will wander right past my humble establishment."

"Smart," Tra'var said.

It was an excellent idea, but Damos took something else away from the conversation. She'd referred to Princess Phaedra Kari by her first name. There was clearly a relationship between the two human females, which likely explained how she had come to be one of the first humans allowed to settle in Haven. Their *mahaya* had connections to what passed for the royal court here on Liberty. He wasn't sure how he felt about that.

It was good to hear Anya speak about the colony so

inclusively, though. She spoke with conviction and determination instead of merely paying lip service to the idea of acceptance and community. If her heart was as open as her mind, maybe this could work.

Maybe.

5
______

Anya stepped out of the winter air and into a shop that would have been cozy if the décor hadn't been entirely made of metal—much of it in sharp and pointed shapes.

She drew her arms a little closer to her sides and resisted the urge to touch the gleaming blades that filled more than half the room.

She recognized the layout of the building immediately. It was common in many of the pre-fab homes that housed most of the colony. They were in what should have been the main living area, only in this case the walls had been removed or omitted during construction. Where the kitchen should have been was a small, well-lit workspace full of tools. Many projects were in progress, but she was too far away to make out any details.

Both males stood behind her, watching silently as

she moved through the space. When she got more comfortable, she touched the hilt of a dagger with a gem-encrusted handle and a blade no wider than her pinkie finger. "Form over function?" she asked almost absently and then froze when she realized how insulting that sounded. "I mean. It's beautiful. Really. But how do you hold it without cutting your hand?"

"You don't." Damos smiled as he picked up the weapon and held it up so she could see it better. "Only the point is sharp, not the edge. It's meant to decorate a female's hair."

He made a vague gesture around the back of his head with his free hand. "To help pin it up. Originally they were also for defense, but the females at court don't fear attack, so these became a fashion statement instead of a weapon."

"This is a hairpin? Can I try it?"

"Of course," they both said at almost the same moment.

She pulled her hair out from under her cloak and let it fall down her back. She was about to start twisting it into a simple chignon when she realized both males were staring intently. She wasn't even sure they were breathing. Had she committed some kind of cultural sin that Saral hadn't remembered to warn her about?

"Something wrong?"

"Your hair is beautiful. I didn't realize it was so long," Tra'var said.

"Or that it was the color of *asloni vren*." Damos'

amber eyes gleamed brightly, the dark rims showing up starkly in contrast.

"Cold steel?" she asked, trying not to feel self-conscious as she struggled to translate Damos' words.

"Cooling steel," he clarified in Galactic Standard.

"Ah." She winked and held out a lock of her hair. "I thought you were commenting on the amount of silver in my hair. Another decade or so and it *will* look like cold steel."

Damos shook his head, but Tra'var spoke first. "You will look just as you do now. Your nanotech will see to that."

Time for revelation number one. Anya bowed her head so she didn't have to look at them. She focused on twisting her hair up so she could try the dagger in it. "I don't have nanotech. I'm just a basic model human. No upgrades."

Tra'var made a startled noise and then demanded, "Why not?"

She had an answer prepared for the question, and she rattled it off without stopping what she was doing. "I have a unique contract. I had no idea if the tavern would be successful, so I made a deal with the council. I stay for three years. If I decide this is where I want to stay, I can take the nanotech treatment. Until then, I have all the rights as an ordinary citizen of Haven."

"No," Tra'var stated flatly.

Anya took the dagger and slid it into her hair before she looked up. Tra'var's expression was stormy. "What do you mean, no?"

"You will not wait three years. You are our *mahaya*. You will carry our nanotech soon." He folded his arms across his chest and gave her a look that had her ready to reach for the dagger she'd just slid into her hair.

She glowered up at him. "No."

Tra'var cocked his head in confusion. It would have been adorable if she wasn't so *fraxxing* annoyed.

"No what?" he asked.

"No to anything you said that started with the words 'you will.' I may be your *mahaya*, but that doesn't give you the right to tell me what to do." She turned to glare at Damos. "Either of you."

"But you are our—" Tra'var didn't get to finish the sentence before Damos cut him off.

"You are right, Anya." Damos raised both of his massive hands, palms out, fingers splayed. "The choice is yours."

"Damn right it is. I'm not giving up my life or my plans just because our chemistry is compatible. I am not a slave to my pheromones." She frowned. "Or is it your pheromones? Whichever. Biology and chemistry are not in charge of my life."

Tra'var's mouth opened and then shut with an audible click.

Anya pulled the dagger out of her hair and handed it back to Damos. "Word of advice, Tra'v. Don't annoy your *mahaya* when she's standing in a display room full of weapons."

Tra'var lowered his head, ran a hand through his blond hair, and then looked at her askance. His expression was one of perplexed frustration. "You are... not what I expected."

She laughed, and all her annoyance melted away. "You're still light years ahead of me. I wasn't expecting you two at all."

"A fact we both need to keep in mind." Damos reached out and then paused before his hand got too close to her. "May I? Your hair is..."

She tipped her head to one side and drew the length over her shoulder so that it spilled down her front instead of her back. Her hair was her one vanity. She didn't wear cosmetics and was well past the age of dressing for attention. She preferred comfort to the latest fashions, especially when it came to footwear. It was gratifying to know she wasn't the only one who liked her hair.

Both males crowded closer, twining locks of her hair around callused fingers. "It's so soft," Tra'var said.

Damos didn't speak. He stroked her hair like it was a living thing. His jaw moved just a little and she recognized the movement. He was subvocalizing on the comms implants the Vardarians used.

"What did you just say to Tra'v?" she asked.

Tra'var grinned. "If you had an implant, you'd know already."

She rolled her eyes. "You know I can't get one until I have nanotech, and we already had that conversation." She changed the topic before he could respond. "So, what did he say?"

To her amusement, Tra'var pressed his lips together and then shook his head.

"It's a secret. You'll find out later," Damos said. Then he wrapped a length of hair around his fist and pulled her in for a hard kiss that made her toes curl and her heart race. Damos was all rumble and growl, the sound rolling through her body and buzzing against her lips as his mouth slanted over hers.

Liquid heat pooled deep in her belly, and she squeezed her thighs together to try and ease the ache between her legs. Her clit throbbed in time to her pounding heart as the slow-burning embers of the *sharhal* ignited once more.

She kissed him back, craving the heat of his mouth and smoky, sinful taste of his lips.

A moment later, Tra'var caught her by the shoulder and turned her toward him, stealing her from Damos to claim a kiss of his own. His mouth was so hot it was like a brand against her skin, and when he nipped her lower lip, demanding entrance, she whimpered and opened to him.

"No biting," Damos said.

Tra'var stopped to snarl something unintelligible at Damos and then his lips crashed down on hers once more. His arm locked like a steel bar across her lower back, pressing her against him from hip to breast. *Re'veth*, the two of them should have their mouths registered as lethal weapons. Her hands moved over the powerful wall of his chest and she revised her last thought. They should have their whole damned *bodies* registered.

All her plans to take this slow and learn more about her would-be lovers melted faster than ice in a steam bath. Now she was near them again, the *sharhal* had returned full force, and she couldn't even remember why giving in to it wasn't the best idea she'd ever had.

Tra'var had never met such a beautiful, glorious, obstinate female. What had his ancestors been thinking when they'd joined her life to his? He'd dreamed of a soft, gentle female. They'd sent him one already forged in flame, with edges sharper than any blade he and Damos had ever crafted.

Despite his confusion he wanted nothing more than to kiss her until she softened and the walls around her heart melted away. Then he would tear off her clothes and make her scream with pleasure. They'd fuck her until she stopped fighting this, and then... then they'd claim her completely. Mating marks on her throat and their *harani* on her arm.

Once she understood what it meant to be their *mahaya,* the rest would fall into place. Home. Family. Offspring. Damos thought she needed more time. He didn't agree with his *anrik.* All she needed was to be shown what the future would be like for the three of them, and he knew just where to start—once he'd finished kissing her, that is. That could take a while.

Her scent wrapped around him like a caress and every breath drew more of it into his lungs. The more of her he had, the more he wanted. Taste. Touch. Scent. Her soft gasps and moans as their tongues danced and their bodies pressed together. Her fingers stroked the back of his neck, holding on to him just as tightly as he held her.

The only reason he stopped was the soft chime of their resident AI. He lifted his head and sighed.

Damos walked out of the back room a few seconds later, holding the wrapped bundle of *kes'tarvs* they were supposed to deliver today.

"Already?" Tra'var grumbled. He'd lost all track of time. He'd also missed the moment Damos had left them alone, and that didn't sit well with him.

"Time moves faster when you're enjoying yourself." Damos put the weapons into a carry bag and set it on the floor. "In fact, you're going to be late unless you wing it. You two should hurry."

"You're not coming with us?" Anya asked.

His jaw tightened for a moment before Damos shook his head. "I can't fly that far."

Anya pulled out of Tra'var's arms. He let her go, but she wasn't fast enough to catch Damos before he turned and walked back through the door to the storage room.

Anya stopped, her hands opening and closing as she looked first at the door and then back at him.

"You upset Anya," he sent to Damos as he moved

to their *mahaya's* side and took her hand in his. "It's not you. I'll explain soon," he told her.

"The two of you need some time together, and I have work to do. Is that hilt you made back here somewhere? The one we talked about, with the fire stone in the pommel?" After a brief pause, Damos added. *"You need to get moving or you're going to be late."*

"Funny that. I know I set that reminder to go off early enough we could walk."

Damos didn't respond. He didn't have to. Tra'var knew he'd changed the reminder so there wouldn't be enough time to get there without flying. He'd have to confront his partner about that later.

"The hilt is on my workspace. Back left corner. It's ready to go, just needs the blade."

He already knew what Damos had planned. It was the secret they were keeping from Anya. They'd worked on the blade together this morning, but it wasn't finished yet. He hadn't expected to be left alone with Anya while Damos finished the dagger on his own.

"Is this about his wings?" Anya asked, her voice barely more than a whisper.

He should have known. Gossip moved at close to light speed in a place as small as Haven. All he said was, "Yes. But later." This wasn't a conversation he wanted to have within earshot of Damos.

"Later," she agreed, her tone making it clear that he didn't have long before the topic would come up again.

"So, how is this going to work? You fly these over and I'll meet you there? Where are we going, anyway?"

"The main practice arena. I am not leaving you to walk there on your own. I'll carry you."

"You're joking. I'm not exactly a featherweight at one G, and this is a higher gravity world. If you're holding me and all that," she flicked a hand toward the *kes'tarvs*, "how are you even going to get airborne?"

"Come over here and I'll show you." Tra'var picked up the bag and then placed the carry-strap over his head so that it crossed his body while leaving space for his wings.

Anya hadn't moved.

"Come," he repeated.

Anya made an unimpressed noise at the back of her throat and pointed up. "One little problem. There's a ceiling in the way. You might be the buffest flyer on the planet, but even you can't take off from here. Also, I'm not sure what the context of your last command was, but either way, it doesn't work like that with human women."

"Noted, my lovely *sandar*. You're right about the ceiling. I just wanted to show you what I planned before we went out into the cold again."

Her lips quirked into a bemused smile. "Ah. You should have just said so. And what's a sandar?"

"A desert flower on my home world. Fragrant and beautiful." And guarded by spines as long as a male's thumb, but he didn't mention that detail.

She stepped in front of him. "So, what do I do? Is

there a safety harness I should put on? Do I need a parachute?"

"You trust me," was all he said and then scooped her into his arms.

Anya yelped in surprise and threw her arms around his neck. "Holy *fraxx*, this is the plan? If you drop me..."

"I won't. If I let anything happen to you, Damos would throw me into the forge and I wouldn't try to stop him. You're our future, Anya." He tipped his head so he could look into her hazel eyes. "You are our *everything.*"

Her eyes widened and a soft gasp fell from her lips. He knew it was because of the *sharhal* as much as his words, but that didn't matter. She was beginning to understand.

Confident that things were progressing as they should, he carried her through the shop and storage areas. The door opened automatically when it sensed him, letting him walk into their backyard.

Damos was already at work. He'd shed his cold weather gear, opting to work shirtless. He was so close to the forge his scales had tightened, including the dorsal ridges that ran between his wings.

The stubborn male had done that on purpose, deliberately letting Anya see another of his differences. Damos thought of them as flaws, and nothing Tra'var said could make his *anrik* change his *qarfing* mind.

Anya didn't react at all save for a tiny scowl that was gone almost as quickly as it appeared. Then she raised her voice to carry over the noise of the forge. "Damos, we're going, but before we do I want to check on something. As much as I enjoy ogling your ass, please turn around for a moment."

Tra'var shook with barely suppressed laughter as Damos stiffened and then turned, looking more than a little confused. Clearly he'd expected their *mahaya* to have a different reaction than the one he'd gotten.

"What do you want to know?" he asked.

"Two things. One, is this really a safe way for Tra'var to carry me or am I being played for a fool? Two, would you really stuff him in the forge if he dropped me?"

"I already answered that," Tra'var reminded her, stung.

"And I'm getting a second opinion," Anya retorted.

"He could carry me if he had to... and if I allowed it. You are perfectly safe. And yes, if he let you come to harm, I would consider using his worthless hide as fuel." Damos grinned, flashing his fangs. "But only if you asked me to."

"Right. Pretty sure that's never going to happen, but good to know," Anya drawled. "Oh. One more thing. I am not leaving without a goodbye kiss. You left before I could give you one earlier."

Yes. She was making her acceptance as clear as a summer sky.

"If you smile any wider your face will crack," Damos sent to him via their private link.

"She has accepted us. Soon we'll mark her and finalize the claim. You were worried over nothing."

Damos ignored him, but he didn't disregard Anya's request. He left the forge to do its work and crossed the snow-covered yard. He tucked a finger under their *mahaya's* chin, lifted her head, and then kissed her softly. "Enjoy your time with Tra'var. I will be here when you return."

"Then will you show me what you're making?" she asked.

"Of course," Damos said in a voice that was more contented rumble than actual words.

Tra'var had never heard his *anrik* sound so happy before, and they'd been bonded since they were boys.

"Then later, you can both give me the tour." She touched Damos' cheek and then turned her head to smile at Tra'var. "Okay, Tra'v. Time to prove me wrong."

"Take care of her," Damos spoke on their link as he stepped back to give them room.

"Of course," Tra'var sent back. Then aloud he said, "You might want to hold a little tighter. I've never quite gotten the hang of take-offs."

Anya's eyes narrowed and her arms locked around his neck. "Not funny."

He laughed, spread his wings, and then took to the air, his pride and nanotech working hard to ensure it was a perfect launch. Within a few wing beats they were climbing into the winter air, rising in circles to a comfortable height for over-city flying.

"He was kidding about the take-offs. Don't trust him on the landings, though!" Damos called a moment before they passed out of earshot.

"He exaggerates. I dropped him *once* and he's never forgiven me."

"From how high?" Anya asked, making an obvious effort not to look anywhere but at him.

"Less than a meter..." he paused and then admitted, "into a river. In the middle of the winter. There was ice involved."

She laughed. "I can see why forgiveness hasn't been offered. You dump me in an icy stream, and I'll be doing more than carrying a grudge, though."

"Noted. It was an accident, though. I thought I was strong enough to carry him. Back then, I wasn't... and he'd never gone flying before."

"Never?" she had to raise her voice to be heard over the wind now.

He shook his head but didn't say anything more.

Anya nodded and then pointed to the ground with her brows raised in question. They'd talk about it after this flight.

They needed to learn so much about each other and had so many plans to make.

He couldn't wait to get started.

6

———

She was flying.

The strangest part was the lack of noise. The wind sang in her ears but that was it. There was no engine. No seating. She didn't even have a *fraxxing* safety harness. Anya loved it.

The cold air nipped at any bit of exposed skin and made her eyes water, but she just blinked the tears away. It took her a little while to get up the courage to look around, but once she did she found so much to look at that she forgot to be nervous.

"It's so pretty!" she raised her voice so Tra'var would hear her over the wind.

The colony was blanketed in snow that sparkled whenever the sun managed to break through the cloud cover. She'd never seen anything like it. The sea was a moody gray-blue in the distance, mirroring the dark clouds rolling in from offshore. She didn't know much about terrestrial weather patterns yet, but she knew what that meant. Another storm was coming.

"More snow?" She looked back at Tra'var and then pointed to the clouds.

"Looks like it." Tra'var inhaled. "Smells like it, too."

She had no idea what he meant, but since talking was hard, she tried it for herself instead of asking. She breathed in, the air cold enough she could feel it chilling her nasal passages. Huh. The air *did* smell different.

She felt rather than heard Tra'var laughing. Then he said near her ear. "I told you so."

"Trust but verify," she retorted. It was one of her mother's favorite expressions.

Tra'var grunted. "You should always trust me." A moment later his arms tightened around her as he pulled his wings in closer to his body.

They fell out of the sky like a ship with a dead engine.

"Asshole!" she hollered and then buried her face against his shoulder. She trusted him not to kill her, but she didn't need to watch their descent, either.

The moment he set her down, she pulled away from him. At least, she tried to, but her legs wobbled, and her brain was still convinced she was airborne. When she stumbled backward and would have fallen, he caught her and drew her back into his arms.

"I'm sorry, my *mahaya*. I shouldn't have done that."

"I'm fine. Just a little unsteady. I'm not used to

doing power dives without a spacecraft being involved." She pushed on his chest, but she could have been trying to shove a planet out of orbit for all the good it did. "You can let go now."

He touched her cheek with one callused finger. "I'd rather not."

She huffed at him. "That's not fair. I'm trying to be mad at you right now and you're making it really difficult."

His answering smile was sweet, sexy, and just the slightest bit smug. "Good."

"Ass."

"Yeah. I was. I just..." His expression slipped, and for the first time she got a glimpse of who he really was behind the cocky attitude and easy smile. He looked uncertain and vulnerable. It wasn't what she'd expected. Men were men no matter their species, and she'd never known one to drop his guard like this.

She gave him a few more seconds to finish the sentence. He didn't.

"You just what? Talk to me, Tra'v."

His expression turned sheepish and his wings drooped a little. "It bothers me that you don't trust me yet."

"I have news for you, tall, blond, and shiny. If you want to earn someone's trust, don't go into a steep dive the first time they go flying with you."

He hung his head so she couldn't see his face. "Logic isn't helping me feel better."

This time when she stepped away, he let her go. "I'm not doing this to improve your mood."

Her words came out sharper than she intended, but maybe that wasn't a bad thing because his head snapped up and he met her gaze. "No, you're not. And that is..." he grimaced. "You're not what I expected."

"So you've mentioned. Welcome to the universe as I know it. Nothing is ever what you think it's going to be. Doesn't mean the situation is any better or worse than before. It's just different." She could have said a lot more on the topic, but now wasn't the right time. Besides, this was his moment of doubt. She'd have her turn later.

"Different. Yes." His smile returned, warmer than before. "Definitely not worse, though. I know that much already. Will you forgive me?"

She took his hand. "Just promise me no more dives without permission from your passenger."

He touched his free hand to his chest and then raised it in a gesture like he was offering something up to the sky. "I swear by the breath in my lungs that I will never do that again. May the ancestors witness this vow."

She wasn't sure what to say to that, so she repeated something she'd heard done by other Vardarians at her bar. "Witnessed," she said slowly in his language, making sure to get the pronunciation correct.

It must have been the right thing to say because he grinned and nodded. "You know so much about our ways already."

"Not as much as it seems. That was just something I heard at the bar often enough I asked what it meant. It took me a while to learn it, too. Some words still tie my tongue into knots every time I say them."

A look of dark longing flashed in his eyes and his smile turned into something almost predatory. "Do not injure your mouth, *mahaya*. I have plans for it later."

Her brain cells short-circuited and her witty retort died unspoken, replaced with a single breathy word. "Yes."

"*Atarflorinti*," he murmured. His talented tongue clearly had no problem wrapping itself around the word.

"Did you just witness my agreement?"

"Yes I did."

"And that means you're marking what I said and will hold me to my word. Right?"

"Exactly." He kissed the tip of her nose.

"No one warned me how tricky you Vardarians are. That really should be in the introductory guide."

He blinked. "What guide?"

"The one all the human colonists are given. Cultural differences, beliefs, even a historical overview." She waggled her brows. "Oh, and courtship rituals. Maggie sent me a copy this morning. I haven't had time to read most of it." It was even more expansive than the article Saral had sent."

"Is there one on your species?" he asked immediately.

"Uh. No idea. Saral didn't mention one." She

hadn't planned on revealing that Saral was the source of most of her information about the Vardarians.

"You've spoken to Saral about us?"

"I may have asked her a few things." She cast about for a way to redirect the conversation. "Shouldn't we be going inside? You have a delivery to make. Don't want to be late." And she really didn't want to discuss what she'd learned from Saral and N'tev during last night's conversation. They were having enough trouble keeping their hands off each other as it was. Admitting she'd had a blunt conversation about the ins and outs of physical intimacy with an alien species would only add rocket fuel to the fire.

"You're right. We have places to be. Warmer places. Perhaps we should walk back. I wasn't expecting the wind to be so cold."

"I didn't notice. Then again, I was a little distracted. That's the first time my feet have been off the ground without a vehicle being involved."

"But not the last." Tra'var draped a possessive arm across her shoulders and led her toward a pair of massive doors. "Have you been to one of the arenas before?"

"Not yet. I mean, it's a training and fitness facility. It would be rude to just wander in and gawk at all the pretty males working out. Right? Or is that a human thing?"

"That is definitely a human thing. Females often attend to enjoy the view and select potential partners for uh... short-term enjoyment."

She barked out a laugh. "Is that what you call it? Because at the bar, we just call it a hookup."

He stopped walking and then shrugged. It wasn't quite the same as the human version, but it was close. He lifted one shoulder and dropped the other while his wings mirrored the motion. "I was being circumspect. Given your occupation, I suppose I shouldn't have worried."

"*Fraxx* no. I'm sorry, Tra'v, but the ancestors sent you a mate who curses in multiple languages and has heard things that would make an angel weep and the devil blush."

He frowned. "What is a devil?"

"I'll explain demon and angel mythology to you another time." She inclined her head toward the doors, which were only a few steps away. "Now I'm curious to see what I've been missing out on."

She'd seen some of the practice centers from the outside even though she'd never been inside one before. This was the largest one in the colony, a massive circular structure that took up nearly an entire block of space. The walls were solid at the bottom, but the upper levels had openings and archways large enough for Vardarians to fly through. It had no roof, just an energy shield that encapsulated the entire building, keeping out the elements while still allowing beings to push through with only minimal resistance.

They walked through the barrier and on toward the doors. The moment they were inside the bubble, the winter chill gave way to a more temperate climate.

There was no snow on the ground, and her breath no longer turned to vapor when it hit the air.

She hadn't realized the shield acted as a sound dampener, too. Now that she was on the other side, she could hear the clang of weapons and shouting in at least two languages.

Sand grated beneath her boots, and she glanced down at the tiled floor in confusion. Where was the sand coming from?

The answer came a moment later when several servo-droids appeared from slots in the walls and started to sweep the entranceway, pushing the debris toward a large opening that led to the practice area. The floor was covered in golden sand. It reminded her of old vids about gladiators from human history.

Tra'var touched his hand to a scanner, registering the two of them as spectators.

"Thank you for making it clear that I am not here to get my head handed to me," she said.

"No one would dare. You may not yet wear our *harani*, but you are our mate and I would not let them touch you."

"*Harani*. Those are the armbands that mark a mated trio. Right?"

"They are." He gave her a hot-eyed look. "I look forward to the day you agree to wear ours." His voice dropped to a murmur. "And nothing else."

Her cheeks burned hot enough to rival a star and a very different kind of heat pooled low in her belly, making her ache with need. "Behave," she hissed at him.

Tra'var just inhaled deeply and then grinned at her. "Why would I do that when teasing you increases your pheromones? You smell delicious."

"Because we are in public. And uh... I haven't agreed to this insanity yet."

"But you will. Soon. Because that feeling burning inside you right now, I know it well. Damos and I feel it too."

If they kept talking about this, she was going to do something reckless and hormonal that she would regret later. So she pulled her cloak off over her head, taking longer than usual to free herself, just so she didn't have to reply or even look at him.

Maturity. Maybe next lifetime she'd develop some. Maybe.

Once the cloak was off, she found Tra'var standing close by with one hand outstretched. He'd managed to strip off his own outerwear and had it neatly draped over his arm.

"I'll put these in a locker. That way you won't get overheated from carrying your cloak around with you."

The smug asshole knew damned well that wasn't why she was running hot. Not that she was admitting that to anyone. Especially not him.

She handed her things over. "Thanks. It really is quite warm in here."

"Quite," he agreed with such droll humor she

briefly considered prodding him with one of the *kes'tarvs* he carried.

Not that she knew how to use one. Maggie had showed her the one Striker had given her as a gift, but that was the only time she'd really gotten a good look at one. They weren't a common weapon, so a large delivery like this would mean a group was...*ah*.

That's why they were here. The *kes'tarvs* must be for the newly formed band of rangers Striker had agreed to lead and train. She'd heard the buzz about that last night before her destiny had waltzed through the door of her bar and knocked her ass over afterburner.

If the rangers were here, then so were Maggie and Striker. It was time to face her friends for the first time as a claimed woman. Semi-claimed? Definitely not single but still in denial? Something like that.

"Once we step onto the sand, stay close to me and keep an eye out for falling objects," Tra'var said calmly as he returned to her side.

"You mean like dropped weapons?"

"And the occasional unconscious body."

She slid an arm around his waist and leaned into him. His vest had two splits in the back to allow his wings to extend, which meant she was touching more bare skin than fabric. It was going to make the *sharhal* worse, but better an itch she couldn't scratch than a Vardarian landing on her head.

"I will not let anything happen to you." She expected him to put an arm around her shoulders, but he extended a wing instead, curving it around her body in a surprisingly comfortable embrace.

They entered the arena floor, and though several curious glances came her way, everyone around them was too busy sparring to pay much attention. Blades flashed and chimed all around her, even in the air above her head. Warriors dove and spun, battling each other with a variety of weapons—knives, swords, a few *kes'tarvs*, and even something she thought was called a crossbow.

Tra'var ignored the chaos, guiding her across the sand to a quieter area where a group was assembled.

She recognized some of them immediately. Maggie and Striker. Wreckage and Ruin. There was another cyborg she didn't recognize and standing beside them was... "Is that a human? A *male* human? When did we get one of those?" she asked Tra'var, keeping her voice low.

Tra'var scanned the group and then scowled. "That's Cameron, the only survivor from the mercenary ship that tried to take Maggie and Jade. I guess he's allowed to leave his quarters now."

"Wasn't he some kind of prisoner or something? Nothing to do with the mercs?" Now that Tra'var had identified him, Anya recalled a few details she'd heard in passing. Maggie had mentioned him, but Anya had been more concerned about her friend's abduction and escape than hearing about some random stranger.

"They won his contract as part of a debt." Tra'var

glanced down at her. "I hadn't realized slavery was still permitted in this part of space."

"Technically it isn't. That doesn't stop the corporations and plenty of underhanded jerks using indentured service as a workaround. If the being gets paid, it's not slavery. At least, that's what they keep insisting."

"You don't agree?" he asked.

She didn't hold back. "I think it's a vile, barbaric practice that should be outlawed. Every being deserves to be free. I'm one of the lucky ones. My family worked off their corporate debt generations ago. We'll never go back to a life of servitude. Never."

Tra'var made a soft sound of approval, but before he could say anything an ear-piercing squeal of delight tore through the air. "Anya! You left and Saral wouldn't say anything and holy *fraxx* why are you even out in public? Shouldn't you be doing the mating fever thing?" Maggie didn't stop asking questions as she ran straight for Anya, grinning.

"Do you need assistance, or shall I assume this is a friendly charge?" Tra'var murmured.

"Just make sure she doesn't knock me on my ass. I swear she's gotten stronger since she took the medi-bot treatment."

"Of course. It's part of the process. You'll experience it for yourself soon enough."

Maggie's enthusiastic hug saved Tra'var from a sharp reminder that she hadn't agreed to that. He still didn't understand that, for her, choice was important.

Even if it was just the illusion, she needed to feel like she had options.

"You okay?" Maggie whispered as she squeezed Anya. She had switched to a Terran trading patois they'd discovered wasn't included in the Vardarian translation matrix.

"All good. Just trying to adjust to my new reality," Anya replied in the same dialect.

"Striker says they're good males and I shouldn't worry."

"They are. I think. It's just... I knew it was possible, but the odds were... and now here I am."

"Enjoy. And if you need us, we're just a message away." Maggie gave her one last squeeze and then released her. The feisty redhead turned her attention to Tra'var, stating in Galactic Standard, "I know you helped save Jade and me, but if you hurt my friend, I will still find a way to make you regret it."

Tra'var bowed his head. "Witnessed."

Okay. That was not the response she'd expected. Tra'var had taken Maggie at her word and, if she was grasping the situation correctly, had just acknowledged Maggie's threat and accepted the consequences. That was comforting in an unsettling sort of way. "But not without my say-so," Anya added.

Maggie laughed. "Witnessed."

Tra'var shifted the bag on his shoulder. "Your weapons are here. Shall we proceed?"

"In a hurry?" Maggie asked.

Tra'var was surprisingly blunt. "Yes. The *sharhal* is

intensifying and I would prefer to be alone with my *mahaya*. Soon."

"That's so romantic!" Maggie smiled and then led them over to the others.

Striker made introductions, though she knew most of them by name already. The big silent cyborg was called Axe. He reminded her of Raze, the cyborg who had originally founded the colony. He had the same weathered look—craggy features, long black hair, and a beard that looked like it had been trimmed with a knife instead of scissors.

Four other Vardarians were present. Darz and Vyrn were unmated males she'd seen at the tavern from time to time. The other two were Saral's son B'ron and his *anrik*, Kotar. They were young by Vardarian standards, though they looked to be in their mid-twenties to her.

They gave her a polite nod of greeting, but most of their attention was on the only human male most of them had ever seen.

"And this is Cam. He's expressed an interest in joining us for training," Striker finished the introductions.

Kotar snorted and said in Vardarian. "No nanotech. No wings. He doesn't even have a translator implanted yet. How are we supposed to work with him?"

Striker growled, his tone suddenly one of command as he barked in Galactic Standard. "Because

I am ordering you to. If you don't like it, see yourself out. Everyone here is a volunteer."

Maggie stamped her foot and then pointed at Kotar. "Don't be a speciesist asshole. You were born in a free society with advanced technology. Cameron and I didn't have that luxury."

The young Vardarian blinked. "Uh. Right. Sorry." He looked at Cameron and switched to Galactic Standard. "Welcome to the colony. We're uh, looking forward to working with you."

Cam laughed. "Yeah. I can tell. And I'm not really part of the colony yet. I'm on probation. I even have a pair of babysitters to make sure I behave." He jerked a thumb toward Wreckage and Ruin.

"We're not going to sit on you. Who sits on an infant?" Ruin demanded. "Why are humans so strange?"

"It's in the handbook. And no, we can't show it to you. If we did, we'd have to burn that one and issue a new one," Anya stated.

Maggie and Cam laughed. Everyone else stared at her.

"I can't tell if you are joking or not," Tra'var said quietly. "It's disconcerting."

"Good." She pointed to the others. "Don't you have weapons to deliver?"

"I do. And once we're done..."

There was no mistaking the passion that roughened his voice or the way his eyes blazed with heat as he looked at her like she was his favorite snack.

She swallowed hard and nodded, not trusting herself to speak.

Tra'var touched her cheek briefly and then left her to hand out the weapons.

She watched him go, taking a moment to appreciate the predatory way he moved. As he walked away, he folded his wings, shifting the fabric with a twitch of his shoulders so it covered his back again.

She didn't even notice Cameron's approach until he was barely a meter away. He had a smile on his face and held out a hand in greeting. "Hi. I'm Cam. You're Anya. Right? I hear you have the best bar on the planet."

She took his hand and shook it. "I am and I do. You're welcome any time your nannies decide you're allowed out in the evenings."

Cam shot a look over his shoulder at Ruin and Wreckage before looking back at her. "They're good guys. Offered to give me a place to stay and keep an eye on me while I settle in. I get the paranoia. I mean, if I lived in paradise, I'd be careful who I let in, too."

"You like it here?"

The younger man grinned like a child set free in a candy store. "What's not to like? Good food. Free housing. Beautiful women. Better yet, beautiful *single* women."

He lowered his voice. "Is it true that the Vardarians are purely interested in short-term hookups until they meet their mates?"

"It's true. Just treat them with respect and you will

have them eating out of your hand. After all, you're the only pure human male on the planet."

"Yeah, the rest of the men are cyborgs that could break me in half just by looking at me hard enough. The women, though... You think they'd be interested in taking an unmodified human for a test drive?"

Anya burst out laughing. "I think you should remember that the female cyborgs are just as badass as the males. But if you're brave enough..." She nodded toward Maggie. "My bartender doesn't seem to have any complaints."

She didn't know whether to laugh or blush when the brash boy winked at her. "And what about you? Older women are my catnip."

"You're sweet, but no. I'm—"

She felt a rush of wind, saw a flash of metal, and the next thing she knew Tra'var was standing beside her. He had a *kes'tarv* gripped tightly in one hand, the shaft extended to form a barrier between her and Cameron. "She is not for you, human. She's taken."

Cam uttered an undignified squawk and backed up with his hands raised. "Right. Got it. Taken. No looking. No touching. No talking. See? This is me leaving." He gave a faint wave toward her. "Nice to meet you. And for the record, I think you're a hell of a lot braver than I am."

"That was uncalled for!" She turned to glare at Tra'var.

"You are claimed. There will be no flirting with

other males." He raised the stave and then twisted the handle, triggering its collapse. "None."

The weapon vanished back into its sheath and then she was in his arms, crushed against his chest. He took off without warning. Launching them into the air.

"Hey! I wanted to say goodbye at least."

Tra'var didn't say a word until he landed on an empty balcony several floors up. "You will not do that again."

"Oh no. This is not how it works. You may be my *mahoyen*, but that doesn't give you the right to tell me what I can and cannot do." She rose up to her full height and shoved at his chest with everything she had. It wasn't enough to free her, but he seemed to grasp how angry she was because he let her go and then stared down at her in confusion.

"But—"

"No. You can talk in a minute. I'm not done yet. Cameron wasn't my type when I was his age, and he certainly isn't now. But instead of trusting me, you threatened him and pulled me away from my friends. You and Damos are expecting me to accept this whole mated thing without question. I'm just supposed to trust that this is for the best, but you won't even trust me to have a conversation with a male so young he could be my own son!"

She hadn't meant to say this yet, and she really hadn't planned on blurting it out, but she was too angry to engage her filters until it was too late. "Speaking of children, you do realize that I'm too old for that. Right?

I don't know how Vardarian biology works, but with humans it's pretty damned simple. No more eggs, no more kids. I'm too old to have many left, if any. So if you wanted children, you are shit out of luck. Your *mahaya's* baby factory is closed."

She dashed away a stray tear with a shaking hand and looked up at him. "Still sure that your ancestors knew what they were doing when they threw us together?"

7

"No." It wasn't what he should have said. It wasn't even what he *meant* to say. Anya was wounded and hurt, the pain in her eyes flaying him down to his soul. He should have said something comforting and kind, even if it was a lie.

She stilled, all the anger draining out of her in a heartbeat. "Welcome to the club."

"I don't understand. Why would the ancestors..." he trailed off. Finishing that sentence wouldn't help the situation.

"Maybe you should ask them. I have no *fraxxing* idea. All I know is that babies or not, if you don't trust me, this won't work. I'm not going to stop speaking to my patrons or my friends because they happen to be male." Her tone softened. "If that's even going to be an issue now you know I can't make you a father."

"My species bond for life. As far as we can

ascertain, humans, even ones bonded to our kind, do not. This is hard to accept. All of it is hard to accept." He let his wings droop. "But that doesn't mean I can let you go. You are our *mahaya*. That will never change."

Her lips pressed together in a tight line and then she sighed, exhaling through her nose.

He didn't understand her reaction. He'd just told her that it didn't matter what happened, he'd always be there for her. "What's wrong now?"

A ghost of a smile touched her lips. "Wait, was that supposed to make me feel better?"

"Yes." Though clearly it hadn't done so and he had no idea why not.

"I don't know what you thought you were saying, but what I heard was that no matter how disappointed you are, you're stuck with me."

Frustration rolled through him. "That is not what I meant. You are mine, Anya. Always. Having you in my life will make me happy because that is what the ancestors intended for me. For us."

She huffed softly. "So this is our destiny and that's the end of it?"

"Yes. That's how it is with my species. I'm also a practical male. If something doesn't come out as expected, there are only three choices: adjust my expectations, try to fix the project, or throw it away. I am not throwing you away."

"Fixing something for you means throwing it back in the forge and then hammering the shit out of it," she pointed out in a tone drier than a desert wind.

"I'm not putting you in the forge, either." He held out a hand to her. "But we will have moments where one of us accidentally hammers the other. It was like that when Damos and I were first bonded, but we found our way. Now he is as much a part of me as my shadow."

Anya took his hand and held it lightly, but she didn't move any closer. "Okay. I need you to understand something, though. Just because I am not biologically compelled to never look at another male doesn't mean you have to spend the rest of your life worried I'll cheat on you. I won't. I'm not that kind of person. Until now, I've never been involved with more than one guy at a time."

Her words turned his blood to molten steel. She had never known the touch of two males at once. They would be the ones to introduce her to that pleasure. "Never?"

Her lips twisted into a bitter smile. "When it comes to guys, I'm kind of cursed. I prefer to just screw up one relationship at a time."

"This is not a human relationship. There is no way you can break the bonds between us."

"That's not what Saral said." Her lower lip vanished between her teeth for a second. "I probably shouldn't have told you that."

"You discussed *that* with her instead of us?"

"I needed an unbiased opinion. Well, slightly less biased. She's certain this is the best thing that could ever happen to me."

"It is." He had no doubts and hers confounded and irritated him. So did the fact she'd gone to someone else to talk about their new bond. If she had questions, why hadn't she asked them last night before they'd parted?

"It isn't always. I know Kade's parents don't exactly get along, and they're not the only ones. This system of yours isn't perfect."

"Unhappy pairings are the result of years of deliberately poisonous choices. I won't live my life that way, and I don't believe you would either."

"You believe this is the will of your ancestors. That there is some grand plan." Anya tapped a hand to her chest. "I don't. I think the universe is chaotic and we're left to make our choices as best we can and face the consequences later. You and Damos are clearly well-matched, but that doesn't mean the three of us will be."

That made him laugh. "The first time I met that stubborn son of a *gharshtu* he insulted me and we ended up fighting. He broke my nose and I gave him a black eye. I told my parents it wouldn't work. So did he. My fathers sat me down and told me that I had no choice. This binding would elevate my family's standing at court and improve the fortunes of my other siblings and their children."

Anya blinked. "They traded you for improved status." It wasn't a question.

"Yes, that's basically what happened. Damos' fathers loved him, but once they found their *mahaya* and had offspring with her, the family dynamic shifted. None of the higher-ranked families would even consider binding one of their sons to someone with Damos' flawed genetics. I was the only option."

"He's not flawed!" she protested.

"I agree with you. My *anrik* would not. His birth was the result of a brief relationship with a female of mixed species—Vardarian and Ferrym. His mother left on a scientific vessel shortly after their encounter, unaware she was pregnant. By the time she returned, Damos was too far developed for the standard treatments. His fathers claimed him anyway, but their love was not enough to protect him from the judgment of others."

Her expression softened and her voice lost its edge. "You said his fathers claimed him. What about his mother?"

He shook his head. "She only returned long enough to deliver her son and present him to his fathers. She has never been part of his life."

He expected her to react with shock or anger. Instead, she pressed her lips together and hummed in what sounded like understanding. "My father bailed on me, too. He was gone before I learned how to walk. To be honest, I'm not sure he was around that long, but my mom doesn't like to talk about it."

"Damos doesn't speak about his mother either, though I know he still feels the sting of her rejection." Tra'var suspected Damos' mother's choice to cut all ties to her son was the main source of his *anrik's* issues.

"Yeah. That's not easy to get over." She rubbed a hand to her chest, just over her heart. "But I imagine it took a while for you to come to terms with the fact your family basically used you to leverage their status in society."

"It's the way things work." It wasn't really an answer, but it was true.

She snorted. "No wonder so many of you willingly headed to a strange planet to start over again."

"Indeed. We didn't hesitate. This was the right choice for us." He grinned. "For once, the stubborn *bakaffa* didn't even try to argue with me."

"I can't imagine the two of you fighting. You are so close. I mean, I don't know you well yet, but even I can see that."

"We forged our friendship over time, working through our differences and leaning into our strengths. I wouldn't be the male I am today without him. He is my best friend and my blood-bound brother. You are now part of that bond. We *will* find our way."

"I wish I felt as certain as you do."

He drew her in close, folding his arms around her smaller frame and bowing his head over hers. "If you can't trust the will of our ancestors, can you at least try to trust us?"

"I do trust you. I don't know why, exactly. But I do."

Her soft confession filled him with satisfaction. "That is a good start. I will try to have more patience." He nuzzled the top of her head, letting the scent of her hair fill his lungs. "But it is hard."

His spiky little *sandar* chuckled as she rocked her

body against the hard, aching ridge of his cock. "I noticed."

"*Mahaya*," his tone was part warning, part longing. "If you do that again..."

"I know, but if we do, it would take the edge off this crazy *sharhal* thing." She stroked a hand down his bare flank. "It's getting hard—uh, difficult—to think straight."

He was going to tell her no. Not here. Not where anyone could see them. But then she reached behind him, letting her fingers glide over the patch of skin between his wings, and his higher brain functions ceased operation. He growled her name as his lips crashed down on hers, capturing her soft gasp of surprise with his mouth.

He devoured her, taking what he craved. Her touch. Her taste. The warmth of her body and the sweetness of her mouth. He palmed her ass in his hands and then lifted her off the floor without breaking their kiss.

She shifted her hold, letting go of his back to throw her arms around his neck, her soft noises of need humming against his tongue. She wanted this as much as he did, and all his plans to take things slowly were scattered by the maelstrom of lust howling through his veins.

～

Anya stopped fighting and gave in to her desires. There'd be time for doubts and questions later, but right now, all she needed was Tra'var. He was the only one who could ease the ache inside her. The need for sex was so strong it was impossible to focus on anything else for long.

His skin was different now. She could feel the slight ridges of his scales beneath her palms as she clung to him. One of his fangs grazed her lip, and she remembered something important. With the last of her brain cells, she managed to dredge up two small words, "No biting."

He tensed and his next words were little more than a roughened growl. "Why do you still resist this?"

"Because it's an important moment, and when it happens, you should both be there."

He broke their kiss and for a moment she wasn't sure what his reaction would be. Anger? Frustration? Suddenly she was painfully aware of how big he was and how dangerous. A spike of fear cut through her lustful fog, but then it faded as she saw his face. He was smiling at her with something like wonder.

"You are right, little *sandar*. It will be special and Damos should be part of it." His lips parted and he chuckled ruefully. "The *sharhal* has stolen my ability to think."

"Then let's do something about it. This will help. Right? And it's okay that Damos isn't here?"

"It will help for a little while." He locked gazes with her. "You are sure?"

She wrapped her legs around his hips and ground herself against his cock. "Very."

"Then let's ask him." His voice changed to a soft murmur as he subvocalized to his *anrik*, though he kept his voice loud enough for her to hear. "Damos. Anya is in the thrall of the mating fever. She needs relief but is worried you're not here."

She couldn't hear Damos' response, but Tra'var's reply told her all she needed to know. "Yes, I'll make sure to take care of our *mahaya's* needs. Yes, I remember how. It hasn't been *that* long. See you soon."

There was another pause, and then Tra'var snorted. "Asshole." Then he looked down at her. "He understands. We will all have our time together. Separately and together."

"I just needed to be sure."

"I'm glad you asked." He kissed her. "But I think we are done talking now." He spun them so his back was to the arena. She got a quick glimpse of an aerial battle going on some distance away, but then Tra'var spread his wings and blocked her view. She couldn't see anything anymore, but no one would be able to see her, either.

She'd always been a bit of an exhibitionist. A lifetime spent in close quarters on ships and stations had made her that way, but she appreciated that Tra'var was doing his best to keep her shielded. Modesty wasn't a Vardarian trait, at least not that she'd noticed, so he must be doing it for her.

"You don't need to worry. I'm not concerned about voyeurs," she told him.

He curled his lip back to reveal his fangs. "No one else sees you naked but us. Ever."

She patted his cheek and laughed. "Okay, handsome. Do you want me to stay quiet, too?"

He twisted his lips, his jaw canted to one side as he considered. "No. So long as you scream my name when I make you come, I will allow it."

Anya was so amused by his decree that she suffered a filter failure. "Your name. Got it. I'll try to remember that... Dave?"

He growled and surged forward, not stopping until her back was pressed against a wall with his body firmly wedged between her thighs. He'd maneuvered them into a small alcove that partially screened them from view. His mouth was on hers, hot and demanding, and he made primal sounds that had her blood singing and every part of her aching with need.

His vest offered plenty of access to bare skin, but his pants were out of her reach and she had no idea how they fastened. She gave up trying to undress him and focused on herself. She managed to get her shirt over her head, but then he caught her wrists in one massive hand and held her arms over her head, still tangled in her top.

"Pretty."

She felt the warmth of his breath through the lace of her bra, and then his mouth closed on her nipple, sucking through the dark red fabric. She moaned, his touch triggering a zing of pleasure that flowed through her like electricity. Her breath caught, her back arched, and her panties grew damp with arousal at his touch.

When he lifted his head, the cool air of the arena wafted over the wet lace, making her nipple tighten and sending a flurry of goose bumps across her skin.

"What is that?" he asked as he released her hands.

She freed herself from her shirt and then dropped it. "When we feel cold or aroused, that happens."

He lifted his head, eyes sparkling with curiosity. "Which was it?"

"Both," she admitted.

"Then I will warm you so the next time it happens I'll be certain it is pleasure you're feeling."

"Trust me, you've got that covered."

He took a deep breath and grinned. "I can tell."

She blushed. Actually *fraxxing* blushed.

He stared, fascinated, as a flush of heat traveled up her throat to darken her cheeks. He brushed a kiss over the start of the blush. "Warm. I didn't realize." He took another deep breath and made a low, rumbling sound of approval. "It enhances your scent. I need you, Anya. Now."

"Then you're going to have to put me down."

"I don't like that idea," he grumbled. "If you were wearing Vardarian clothing, this would not be a problem."

"I don't own any."

"You will soon."

She could see they needed to have a conversation

about bossiness and boundaries, but now was not the time. Her need was rising to a fevered pitch and she wanted relief.

She wanted *him*.

Tra'var stepped back just enough to give her space and then lowered her to the floor. He deliberately kept their bodies in contact so the slow slide down his torso made her skin tingle.

The moment she was standing on her own he unsheathed a knife from another pouch and raised it in one hand. "Do not move."

If any other man had done that, she would dump him on his ass and run like hell, but this was Tra'var. She went still, her gaze on the blade in his hand.

He moved slowly, not stopping until the point of the blade made light contact with a spot just below her breastbone. He drew the point upward over her heated skin, triggering another flurry of goosebumps.

Her entire focus was on the touch of that blade, the cool metal gliding over her flesh. It was exquisite and arousing, the hint of danger just enough to make everything more intense. She stopped breathing as the knife reached her bra and he turned the blade so the flat part pressed against her skin. He slid it beneath the cloth and then twisted the blade and drew it toward him in a motion so quick she barely saw it happen. The cloth parted with a slight snap and fell away, leaving her breasts bare.

Even the years she'd spent in lighter gravity before coming to Haven couldn't stop the inevitable sag and softening of her body, but she didn't try to cover herself. She knew what she looked like and what the higher gravity of this world had done to her figure. It was all a part of who she was, and any guy who didn't like what they saw was welcome to take his opinions and go.

Tra'var dropped to his knees, looking up at her like she was his personal Venus, as his wings shifted again to hide them both from view. He altered his grip on the knife and then drew the point down her body slowly, moving it from the valley between her breasts to the rounded softness of her belly, and then down to the band of her pants.

The smart thing to do would be to tell him not to cut them away. She should remind him she'd need something to keep her legs warm on the journey home, but she was hypnotized by the light gleaming on the blade and didn't say a word.

He moved his hand lower, letting the tip slide over the fabric until he was between her thighs. "Open."

That single, roughly spoken word made her head spin and she parted her legs for him. He sliced her pants open along the crotch and then slid two fingers inside. He caught hold of her panties and drew them through the hole he'd made before slicing them, too.

"You're slicing up all my clothes."

"I'll replace them with ones that offer easier access to my beautiful mate's body."

She opened her mouth to make a smartass comment, but then his fingers were inside her and she lost the ability to form words. All that came out was a needy moan. She locked her legs and leaned against the wall behind her, her eyes closed as pleasure swept through her.

He stroked a fingertip around her clit and then across it. The calluses on his finger added an extra layer of sensation to his touch, and she had to grip his shoulders with both hands to keep herself upright.

His first few touches were more of a gentle exploration as he learned what she liked. Every gasp and shiver taught him a little more, and it wasn't long before his fingers moved faster, his touch increasingly confident.

She kept her lips tightly closed to muffle the sounds of pleasure she made, sinking her fingernails into the bare flesh of his shoulders as her control started to fray.

She usually took longer to build up to an orgasm. It might have been the *sharhal* or Tra'var's talented fingers, but whatever it was, things were happening faster and with an intensity that shocked her.

"Tra'v," she whispered in warning. "I..."

He looked up, his expression hungry and eager. "Yes. Come for me. Let me see your pleasure, *mahaya*." He slipped a finger into her channel, curving it to reach the sensitive spot most men she'd been with claimed didn't actually exist.

Tra'var proved them all wrong in the best possible way.

He added another finger, working them in and out

at a pace that stole her breath and made it impossible to do anything but obey. Her orgasm bloomed slowly, her body tensing and her breath exploding from between her lips.

He growled her name and then pressed his thumb hard on her throbbing clit. "Now."

Her release tore through her with an almost brutal intensity. She cried out his name as her lungs emptied and she tumbled into a place of impossible pleasure. She didn't know she was falling until he caught her, wrapping her in his arms and holding her close as she shuddered. One of his thickly muscled thighs was between her legs and she rode him shamelessly, using his body to extend her orgasm as he held her.

She was still trembling when he rose to his feet, taking her with him. He did it without apparent effort, and she wondered how much of that was his nanotech and how much was genetics. They were both bigger and stronger than her, but she'd never felt safer with any male in her life. At least, that's how she felt at the moment. It was probably the damned *sharhal* messing with her gray matter again.

Still out of breath from her orgasm, her breathing was jagged and shallow as he pressed her against the wall. His thigh was still between her legs and he used it to hold her up as he reached between them to free his cock.

Apparently their clothes really were designed for easy access because he was still dressed, but at the same time sufficiently naked to give her plenty of bare skin to caress as he eased their bodies into position.

Need drove her to keep moving, trying to get closer to him and craving his touch. He used both hands to hold her in place and moved his thigh from between her legs, replacing it with his cock.

When the broad head slid into her folds, she uttered a low moan, her hips rocking to guide him to where she needed him the most. He held back, moving slowly, his jaw tight with tension as he merged their bodies with light, shallow thrusts that gave her time to adjust to his size.

"More. Please. I need..." She peppered his mouth with tiny kisses, trying to break his control. She didn't want slow or gentle. Not this time. Her legs tightened around him, pulling him deeper.

He snarled something she couldn't make out, his breath exploding from his chest as he drove himself the rest of the way in a single thrust. His mouth found hers, kissing her hard, their tongues tangled and bodies moving as one.

Every part of her was awash in pleasure and she let it carry her away. This was all that mattered right now. Everything else could wait.

Their kiss deepened, each of them taking what they needed from the other. She caught hold of his collar in one hand and used it to pull herself higher, changing the angle between them. His cock hit a new set of nerve endings and her body pulsed around him as the pleasure intensified.

He groaned her name, the sound so raw it made her shiver.

The dance continued in a game of give and take that took her to the peaks of pleasure and then held her there, stoking the fires of her need so bright and hot it was like standing in the center of a star.

His mouth muffled her soft sounds of pleasure and she made no attempt to raise her voice. She didn't care who heard them, but she also didn't want to share this moment with anyone else. This was their time, a perfect moment she would never forget.

Her nails scored his shoulder, her legs tightening again as she reached the pinnacle. He surged into her, his pace unsteady now and his breath ragged as he thrust into her again and again.

She flexed around him, breathless and wild as she came, her entire body tensed and quaking with the force of her release.

Tra'var groaned and powered into her, pinning her against the wall, his control unraveling as his cock jerked and thickened inside her. He came with a low, guttural sound that rolled through her like thunder and buried himself to the hilt inside her. She clung to him, her mouth still on his, as they rode out the last of their storm together.

When she had breath enough to speak, she lifted her head to smile at him and said, "That was incredible. This *sharhal* thing is intense. I'm going to miss it."

That earned her a low, sexy chuckle. "No you

won't. Didn't anyone tell you? The mating fever fades, but the desire never does."

Holy *fraxx*. "Never?"

He nuzzled her cheek. "It will only get better."

"Then why in the name of gravity are you worried I'd cheat on you two? Not that I would, but if this is what's on offer, no female in her right mind would even think about straying."

He laughed again and then hugged her. "I hadn't thought about that. Remind me the next time I have doubts. Oh, and please feel free to tell Damos that I have not forgotten what to do."

"Oh believe me, I will." She should have stopped there, but her mouth got ahead of her brain again. "And then I'm going to need to do a comparison test. Does it get better when we're all together?"

Heat flared in his deep blue eyes. "From what I have been told, yes. But since we only just found you, it will be a new experience for all of us."

Despite the fact she'd just had two incredible orgasms, her body hummed with fresh desire at the thought of sharing a bed with both of them at once.

Tra'var sensed it and smiled smugly. "You like that idea."

There was no point denying it when he was still inside her and could feel her body's reaction. "Yes."

"Then stay with us tonight. Let us take care of your needs, *mahaya*."

There were a dozen reasons she shouldn't agree.

She had a bar to run. Employees to organize. Menus and events to plan. It was too fast. Too soon. Too much.

Only none of the reasons bouncing around her head were really an issue. Her employees didn't need her to organize them. They could run the place themselves. In fact, Saral had already told her not to come in. And the rest... well... she was half-naked and sticky from having sex against a wall with one of her *mahoyen*. Any argument about going too fast had already fled at light speed.

As he moved away from her, another thought struck. "You're going to have to get our stuff out of the lockers. I am not going anywhere until my newly ventilated pants are hidden under my cloak."

He laughed as he kissed her. "Anything my *mahaya* wants."

His words hit her like a rogue comet, turning her brain to mush again. The time for panic had clearly passed. She'd already made her choice and jumped. Now all that was left was the fall... and whatever came afterward.

If she was going to pancake on the surface of the planet of bad judgment, at least she'd make an impressive crater.

8

———

Damos eyed his handiwork critically, looking for any flaw he might have overlooked. He wanted this blade to be perfect. Of all the daggers he'd created in his career, this one was special. It was for their *mahaya*.

Not that she was theirs yet. And she might never truly belong to both of them. He'd known that for years, and he'd deliberately sent her away with Tra'var to give them time to know each other and remind her he was flawed. She didn't seem to care, but he needed to be sure she understood before things progressed much further. His control was slipping by the hour, which was another reason he hadn't joined them for this delivery. It would give her time to think about what she wanted and how she felt about him.

Tra'var accepted his differences, but what were the chances their *mahaya* would, too? Until meeting Anya, he would have said it was impossible. Now, he had a glimmer of hope, but he'd learned long ago that hope was a dangerous thing to have.

He was still examining the dagger when Tra'var contacted him. *"We're on our way back. She has agreed to stay with us tonight."*

"She has?" It was a good thing they'd spent some time reorganizing their living area last night. Over time, supplies and projects had somehow migrated from the shop to their home. Now their storage areas were stacked to the ceiling, but their living space was tidy. Mostly. *"I'll activate the housekeeping bots."*

"Yeah. Good idea. We'll be back before the top of the hour. Going to hit Tarin's for lunch for the three of us. You want your usual?"

"Please." It seemed wrong to have such a mundane conversation right now. Nothing was normal about this day. It was momentous. Important. And here they were discussing food. He wanted to know everything that had happened, even the parts that would make him envious. Why had she agreed to stay? Was she truly accepting all this so quickly? Forge and flames. If she was staying, he needed to size her *harani* so it would fit her properly.

They had made the set of armbands that all bonded trios wore some time ago, in hopes that they'd find their *mahaya* one day. Tra'var had brought the *harani* out last night and cleaned them, but Damos would polish them again once he adjusted hers to fit. Human proportions were different from Vardarian, and like the dagger, this needed to be perfect.

He had just finished polishing her armband when the gate opened.

"I told you he'd still be out here," Tra'var said loudly, giving Damos just enough time to hide the band back in its box and close the lid.

Then Anya appeared at the gate with a smile on her face. "You did, but I didn't believe you. What madman would be outside when it's freezing cold out here?" She gestured to the gray sky above them. "Aren't you cold?"

"There's no such thing as cold when you work with fire." He nodded toward the forge. "Come over here and warm yourself."

She broke into a jog, running right past him to stop only a step or two away from the forge. "Oh, that's much better." Anya held out her hands to warm them faster.

"You need this too, Tra'v. Nanotech or not, you're not immune to the cold. I saw you shivering on the way back."

Damos gestured to his *anrik*. "Finding our mate has clearly made you weak if you're shivering already." He turned to Anya. "He usually works inside at this time of year. I'm afraid my *anrik* is a little... delicate."

"Oh, I wouldn't say that." Anya's lips quirked into a smile. "He was very robust earlier. And not to worry. He took *very* good care of me, just as you asked."

"Thank you." Tra'var shot him a smug look over Anya's head.

"Even if he did scare the *fraxx* out of me by going

into a dive as we arrived at the arena." She fixed him with a determined look. "Neither of you are allowed to make any more jokes about flying... or landing."

"Witnessed," Damos said.

"Witnessed," Tra'var agreed.

"Now we have that covered. Why are you out here? What was so important you couldn't go with us to deliver the *kes'tarvs* to the new rangers?"

"This." He reached past her to pick up the dagger, catching a heady whiff of her pheromones mixed with the scent of sex as he did so. The combination made his cock punch to fully erect in seconds. He had to force himself to focus on the dagger and what they were about to do when all he desired to was to drag her into his arms.

Once he was back in control, he got on his knees, holding the pose until Tra'var joined him. They offered her the dagger together.

"Oh. Oh!" She took the offered gift with a coo of delight. "This is part of the courtship ritual. Right? Saral mentioned it." She pulled the blade from its simple leather sheath and admired it. "I admit I don't understand the symbolism of your gift, but I accept it."

Tra'var chuckled and got to his feet. "What do you think it's for?"

Damos rose too, his gaze never leaving Anya. Her easy acceptance of their gift was deeply satisfying, and her admiration filled him with pride.

"Poking my *mahoyen* when they get out of hand?"

She made a small prodding gesture that didn't come near either of them.

Damos shook his head. "It represents our promise to keep you safe. You are ours to protect, *mahaya*. A duty we will carry out with pride."

"It's beautiful, practical, and symbolic." She turned the knife slowly in her hands. When the light caught the polished gem in the pommel of the hilt, it glowed like an ember burning inside the stone.

"What is that?" She caressed the smooth surface with wonder. "It's like fire trapped inside smoked glass. It's lovely."

"That is *vartis*," Tra'var said in their language and then repeated it in Galactic standard. You would call it a black fire opal."

"An eternal flame for our shining one," Damos added. It wasn't the most poetic of descriptions, but he was better with metal and flame than words.

She smiled—a deeply contented expression that filled his heart with an unexpected light. "It's beautiful. I will treasure this forever. Is there something I should be saying right now? Some part of this ritual I don't know about?"

"You've already said it," Tra'var told her.

A frown creased her brows. Only for a moment, but he'd seen it. She still had reservations? "What is it?"

"Accepting this gift doesn't mean this is a done deal. Does it? I mean, I know it's most likely going to be because of biology and pheromones and the will of your obviously insane ancestors, but I still have a little time. Don't I?"

Tra'var's expression darkened, his jaw so tight it was a wonder his teeth didn't creak from the strain.

"You have time," Damos said. This was about him. She'd already been with Tra'var, so he had to be the issue she was still coming to terms with. He understood that. In the beginning, Tra'var had struggled too. Their bonding had been arranged by their parents, and it had taken his *anrik* time to get over his anger and resentment.

Anya put the dagger into a jacket pocket and then looked up at him. "Is there anything else to this moment? Hugs? Kisses?"

Her question surprised him, but he wasn't foolish enough to let a chance to hold her escape. "Which would you prefer?"

Her gaze intensified, like she was trying to see all the way into his soul. "Both."

He reached for her, but she didn't wait for him. She stepped in close, placed her small hands on his chest, and then rose on her toes, seeking a kiss.

He gathered her to him and then bowed his head. As his lips touched hers, she whispered so softly Tra'var wouldn't be able to hear. "Thank you for giving me more time, but I need you to know something. You're not what I'm afraid of, Damos."

He kissed her then. Not with the hunger he'd intended, but with a gentle tenderness he hoped conveyed what her words meant to him. He wanted to ask what she was afraid of, but he sensed that was best done when they were alone.

She was warm and soft in his arms, her lips parting with a gentle sigh as she returned his kiss with one as tender as his. Warmth filled him, softening the walls he'd built around his heart.

He tangled his hands in the glorious mane of her hair, wrapping the silken strands around his fingers. It was an intimacy he'd never allowed himself before. Most females he'd spent time with weren't interested in any kind of emotional connection. It was the physical act they wanted and sometimes just the thrill of breaking society's unspoken rules. He was what he'd heard the cyborgs refer to as forbidden fruit, which served as an apt description.

Her tongue slipped into his mouth to dance with his, their bodies rocking together. She let one hand slide down his bare chest and across his ribs. He wasn't wearing a shirt. He rarely did when working near the forge, and it hadn't occurred to him to don one before she returned.

Now he was glad he hadn't. He liked it when she touched him. Skin to skin. Her fingers moved along his spine in a slow caress that filled his loins with heat like molten metal. When she reached his wings, he tensed, but she kissed him harder and kept moving until her hand was between them, stroking over skin so sensitive that every touch made his cock twitch.

No female had ever done that for him. His wings

were testament to his differences, and none of them had wanted to touch them. No one but her.

He growled deep in his throat, a wordless sound of need she seemed to understand. She stroked him again, firmer this time.

He scooped her off the ground a heartbeat later, carrying her into the house as she laughed and kissed him by turns.

"Don't mind me. I'll just turn off the forge and bring in our meal," Tra'var muttered.

Damos managed to make an obscene gesture with one hand without dropping Anya, and then he was inside with an armload of willing female who didn't fear him at all.

"You're really going to leave him out there alone?" she asked.

He fought past the lust fogging his brain. He needed one question answered. "He'll manage. I wanted a second alone with you." He held her cradled against his chest, not wanting to be separated from her yet.

"Okay." Her smile faded a little as doubt crept into her expression. "What is it?"

"If you're not afraid of me, what are you afraid of?"

"Oh. That. It's me. I don't bring much to this relationship besides a smart mouth and a healthy sex drive. I have no nanotech. I'm a simple, ordinary human with a lousy track record when it comes to relationships. Not to mention I'm too old to have kids. Most likely, anyway. Even with the differences between our species, I have to be older than you two. I can't give you the family you deserve."

After a long pause, she added. "I should probably add the fact that I babble under pressure to my list of faults."

"I don't perceive anything you just said to be a fault. Honesty is welcome. It's how Tra'v and I managed to work through our differences." He kissed her forehead. "And I don't care how old you are. When you're ready, you'll have our nanotech to ensure that you live a long, healthy life. I like your smart mouth, and I'm happy to hear you're interested in having sex with us often because, if I'm being honest, I want that, too."

"But I can't have kids."

"You don't think you can. If it's important to you, we can find a way. There are many ways to bring children into our lives."

"And if I said that's not something I'm likely to want?"

Being honest was a relief. "Then that will make it easier for me. I've never intended to have offspring."

"Ah." Anya said softly. "Because you don't want a child to have to face the same bias you did?"

He nodded.

"I don't care about any of that."

"You should. Others will." That's when it struck him. Part of his concern in all this wasn't for himself but for her.

"Pfft," she made an odd sound with her lips. "One

advantage to being older? I've learned not to care about what others think. I am who I am. You're just you. And Tra'var is who he is... unshakeable faith in the divine plan and all. Frankly, I think he might be the weird one in this relationship—or whatever we're calling this."

The idea that Tra'var was the odd one was so strange he didn't know what to say in response. His *anrik* was genetically perfect. He was not. "You think so?"

"Oh, definitely. I mean, I hit him with all of this earlier and he just shrugged it off and said it was the will of the ancestors. That is not normal. At least not by human standards."

"Are you saying I'm more human than he is?" He didn't know whether to be amused, insulted, or flattered.

"Sort of? In the best possible way of course. I mean. You're definitely not human. You have wings, scales, fangs, and claws—all of which I like, by the way. But I feel more comfortable with you." She lowered her voice. "Don't tell Tra'v I said that."

"I won't." He set her back on her feet and then cupped her face in his hands. "I hate to say this, but I think Tra'var is right. Our ancestors really did know what they were doing when they brought us together."

She placed her hands over his, and her smile turned bittersweet. "I hope so because this might be what you and Tra'var were waiting for, but I never imagined this could happen to me."

"Being mated?"

"Being trapped."

Her words hit him like a hammer blow, but he understood, too. He wanted to tell her she was wrong, but he wasn't sure she was. So instead, he kissed her gently and then said. "What can we do to make that feeling fade?"

"I don't know. But if I think of something, I'll let you know."

"Do that." He wished he could fix things for her, but this wasn't as easy as reshaping a tool or putting a new edge on a blade. The only thing he could do was give her time and try to make Tra'var understand why he needed to do the same. The ancestors might know what they were doing, but the three of them were in uncharted territory. It would be best if they explored it slowly.

Malfunctioning verbal filters were why Anya had turned down Phaedra's suggestion that she take a seat on the council that ran the colony. It had doomed more than one romantic relationship, yet neither Tra'var nor Damos had reacted badly to her unfiltered outbursts.

Fortunately their meal went smoothly. The males set out the food while she freshened up in the sanitation room, and once she returned, everything had felt normal. It was almost like an ordinary first date, only there were three of them in the conversation and she'd already had sex with one of them. The only one who seemed bothered by that was her, though. Her human sensibilities were going to take a while to adjust to her new normal.

The food was delicious. She'd tried some of the dishes before, but subtle differences in the preparation and seasoning intrigued her. They ate upstairs, which gave her a chance to see their private quarters while they dined.

There was a small flight of stairs between the two floors, and another led to the roof above. Most Vardarian buildings had roofs that were at least partially flat to allow for takeoffs and landings. Small gardens were common, too. Supplementing each family's food supply with fresh greens and herbs. Next year she planned on adding one to the roof above the Bar None.

Their home was built on the slightly larger scale of most Vardarian places with wide halls and doorways to allow them to move with their wings open, high ceilings, and furniture bigger than what was standard for humans.

After the meal, she helped them clean up, putting the scraps into the recycler and setting the dishes in the cleaning unit. As the three of them worked in companionable silence, she felt oddly at home in their kitchen—and with them.

Part of her was happy to spend the rest of the day with them, but she knew they had work to do, and so did she. If she went to work for a few hours before it got busy, she'd feel more comfortable taking the night off. It was only mid-afternoon, and *sharhal* or not, she had a business to run. The three of them were all self-employed, and that meant they'd have to find a way to juggle their careers and their relationship.

Relationship. It wasn't a word she was accustomed to using, at least not pertaining to herself. It was something other beings had, like families... and children. That last word snuck into her thoughts uninvited. She didn't need kids to be happy. As far as she was concerned, that ship had left orbit years ago. And she was fine with that. Better than fine. Her life was her own. She could sleep in every morning, be her own boss, and live life on her terms. At least, that's what she told everyone, including herself.

There'd been a time when she'd thought differently, but times changed, and some things weren't meant to be.

Old memories and regrets came out of the shadows of her past and she slammed a mental door on them. She did not want to think about that right now. Her miscarriage had been so early the doctors weren't even sure she'd been pregnant, but she'd known she was. She'd felt it in her soul.

All her idiot boyfriend had felt was terror. The moment she'd told the father, he'd bolted so fast he hit light speed without a jump engine. *Coward.*

She was still coming to terms with what her pregnancy would mean when the universe changed its mind. A few days of pain and her life was her own again. No more baby. No boyfriend. She'd moved on the way she always did, doing her best to convince herself that it was for the best.

"I think I should head back to my place for a little while. Check in on the bar, get some work done, and change into something less ventilated."

Tra'var laughed while Damos looked confused. "You didn't tell me your clothing got torn. Are you cold?"

"I'm fine. And it didn't get torn. It got sliced by a certain Vardarian with a sharp knife and no patience."

Damos shot his *anrik* a look somewhere between amusement and outrage. "You sliced up her clothes?"

"I was promised replacements. Vardarian, apparently. Something to do with easy access?" Anya said.

Damos snorted and Tra'var's skin turned a gleaming silver across his cheeks.

"Tra'v, did you just blush?"

"My species does not blush."

"We don't." Damos pointed to his partner. "We do that instead. An involuntary tightening of the fine scales on our cheeks. Usually happens when we are feeling foolish."

"Uh huh. That's a blush, Tra'var Caij. Whatever word you want to use to describe it."

"Damos. You are my *anrik*. My blood-brother." Tra'var clutched his chest in mock betrayal. "Why would you do this to me?"

"Because you cut the pants off our *mahaya* during a snowstorm." Damos looked at her, amber eyes bright and grinning so broadly his fangs showed. "We will buy you new ones, Anya. And not just for ease of access."

Veth. He was sexy when he did the dark and broody thing, but when he smiled, he was truly breathtaking.

"In that case, I'm partial to dark green, silver, gold, and red... and black of course. It's still the most slimming shade."

Both males looked confused. "Why would you need that?"

She opened her mouth to explain about flattering her middle-aged woman-living-in-heavy-gravity body type and then closed it again. They were right. And if she wasn't embarrassed by her curves when she'd been naked with Tra'var not two hours ago, why the *fraxx* should she be when she was dressed?

"Forget I said that. But I still like black."

"Noted," Damos said and then fixed Tra'var with a look so fierce it made her want to giggle. "Isn't it, my impatient friend?"

Tra'v threw up his hands. "Yes, yes. I'll see to that this afternoon. Time away from Anya will be sufficient punishment."

"We're all going to have to suffer without each other's company for a bit. I need to get back to work, and so do you. Discovering your soul mates doesn't mean reality stops for any of us."

"I am done working for the day, which means I can at least escort you home," Damos declared.

His tone was firm, and she got the feeling he wasn't going to take no for an answer. That was fine with her. She wanted to spend time with him. This made it easy. "I'd like that."

"And we will collect you this evening." Tra'var gave her a wicked little smirk. "You may wish to pack for a few days away. Once we have you in our bed, I don't plan on letting you leave again until the *sharhal* passes."

"But work!" she protested automatically, though the thought of spending a few blissful hours or days with her *mahoyen* was a powerful temptation.

"Work can be left to others during this time. That is how this works with our species. This is a time for celebration." Tra'var folded his arms over his chest as if everything was now decided.

She mirrored his stance, drawing herself to her full height, arms crossed, shoulders straight. "I am celebrating. I'm also still reeling from the fact we are now a forever thing, not to mention I own a business that doesn't allow for much free time."

Damos looked from her to his *anrik* and back again. Then he threw back his head and roared with laughter that only got louder when both she and Tra'var fixed him with irritated looks.

"What's so funny?" she asked when his laughter had faded to soft chuckles.

"The two of you are like two blades forged from a single block of metal. Different yet at the core, you are the same. I don't know whether to be grateful or worried that the ancestors have provided me with a mate as strong and determined as my *anrik*."

She eyed the two of them for a long moment and then grinned. "Worried. You should definitely be worried."

9
______

THE WALK back to Anya's place revealed something Damos hadn't considered until now. Anya couldn't fly, which meant they would be walking more often than most of his kind. That was normal for him already, but he'd always felt self-conscious about it. Going forward, that would change. He could walk at his *mahaya's* side without anyone looking at him with pity or unease. Some would even be envious. Females of his species were rarer than the males, and many of the male colonists had come to Haven in hopes of finding a mate among the humans.

His species had no reservations about manipulating their children's genetics, but there were laws against changing an unborn child's gender. To make them strong and healthy was one thing, but the choice to alter their gender belonged to each individual and no one else. Despite the problems it caused their society, this had always been a line they wouldn't cross.

Hand in hand, they walked through the quiet streets of the colony. The snowy weather had dampened the population's desire to leave their homes or businesses, though he was certain every child in Haven was outside right now. They laughed and chased each other through the snow, hurling handfuls of the stuff at each other in both air and ground attacks.

A group of older children flew overhead, carrying a sheet laden with snow between them. They were struggling to stay airborne with it, and he turned to watch as they fought to stay up long enough to dump their arsenal on another group building a snow fort.

"Did you ever do this?" she asked suddenly and then gestured around them. "Play in the snow, I mean. It's hard to imagine you ever being so young and small as they are."

"I did, and I was." Though he'd always been large for his age, another manifestation of his unusual genetics. At least his size had been a deterrent to bullies. They flung their barbs and insults from a distance. "Though we didn't get snow often where I lived. The weather was more temperate than it is here." He glanced down at her. "Did you play with other children like this?"

"Me?" She shook her head. "No. I grew up flying around the galaxy with my mother. Back then she was the first officer on a larger ship—one that had a full crew to share the work and make sure I didn't get into too much unsupervised trouble. I had a lot of honorary aunts and uncles, but no other kids my own age. We almost never went planetside. The ship was too big for atmospheric entry, so the closest I got to experiencing weather was in a sim-pod. I didn't set foot on a planet until I was thirteen, and I barely left the ship that first time. The sky was too big, and my brain refused to trust that the air wouldn't suddenly vanish because there was no containment system."

"Ah. I heard some of the cyborgs had the same problem when they first arrived here. They'd been created and lived their entire lives on that research station."

"Exactly. I suggested they do the same thing my mother did for me. Use sim-pods to help them adjust without feeling like they were in danger. It helped most of them."

"But not all." He knew some of the cyborgs still didn't feel overly comfortable outside yet, and one of their number had been so distressed by life under an open sky she'd snuck away despite the fact none of them were legally permitted to leave the planet.

"No, not all. They're adjusting, though." Anya slapped her thigh. "We've all had things to overcome. When I first got here, the higher gravity was exhausting. It took several rounds of treatments and an unpleasant amount of time exercising to get strong enough to deal with it."

"Nanotech would have made that easier."

She shot him an amused look. "Oh, I know.

Phaedra pointed it out to me several times, but accepting the tech meant staying here for the rest of my life, or however long it took the powers that be to realize that this genie is not going back in the bottle."

His translator struggled to piece together her meaning, but he eventually got the gist. "Would it be so bad to live here forever?" he asked.

"It's not that I don't love Haven. This is paradise. I just hate the idea of having my freedom curtailed. I want to be able to leave if I choose. Like I said before, it's about choice. Once I get that upgrade, that's it. I'm here forever."

"Would that be so bad?" Her words stung, even though he'd heard them before. He understood her feelings, but he still resented her resistance. It wasn't like any of them had a choice in this.

"Yes. No. Maybe?" She uttered a frustrated sigh and raised her free hand in a vague gesture he couldn't interpret. "I'm not saying this very well. I'm sorry. I need a little more time."

"I'll give you as much time as I can, *mahaya*." Since she'd already been with Tra'var, he knew that at least some of her doubts had to be about him. He didn't blame her. All he could do was hope that in time, she accepted him the way Tra'var had. If not... well. He'd always known that might happen. He'd lived on the outskirts of others' lives before, even with his own family. It wouldn't be so bad to do it again.

"Thank you. It means a lot to me that you are

willing to do that." She stopped in the middle of the path and pivoted to look up at him.

"This is not about you, Damos. This is my issue. It's just..." she trailed off and then sighed. "I'll spare you the maudlin details. I'll figure this out. You and Tra'var are good males, sweet and kind. I'd be a fool not to want this." She rose on her toes, caught hold of his jacket, and managed to gain enough height to graze the point of his chin with a kiss. "It's not your fault your crazy ancestors sent you a jaded mate with control issues older than you are."

"You are not that old, and I am not that young. By your measurements I am in the middle of my third decade."

She groaned. "And I'm in the middle of my fourth. It's official. I'm a cougar."

The last word didn't translate for him. "What is a coo-gar?"

"Extinct animal from Earth. Also, old slang for an older woman who takes younger lovers."

"Humans are odd. What difference does a decade make?" He frowned as a more confusing thought occurred. "And what does that mean for the cyborgs? Some of them are only a few years old."

"Huh. I never thought of that. I'll have to tease Maggie about it when I see her next."

"You tease your staff?"

"They're all more like family. And yes, I do. I won't see as much of her for a while now she's training with the rangers too. We worked out a schedule that lets her do both, but it means I only see her on our busiest nights. I'm going to need to hire more staff soon or find someone who knows how to fix my damned droids. I was promised they were consistent and capable. The only consistent thing about them is how often they break down."

"Tra'var might be able to repair them. Or we could toss them in the forge and melt them down to remake them into something useful. Do you need more cutlery?"

Anya tapped her chin with one finger several times and then nodded. "That is a tempting offer. Maybe I'll threaten them with being turned into spoons as incentive to do better."

Their conversation halted as a bitter gust of wind whipped by them. It was heavy with the metallic tang that heralded more snow was on its way and made them both huddle a little deeper into their cloaks.

"Brr. I'm extra thankful you two convinced me to borrow a pair of Tra'var's pants. They might be six sizes too big, but at least they don't have drafts."

"You should have taken your own pants off first. That cannot be comfortable."

Her lips quirked into a brief grin. "If I had taken off my pants while in close quarters with two incredibly sexy males drunk on sex pheromones, we'd still be back at your place and none of us would get any work done today."

"Sexy?" That wasn't a word he'd ever heard used to describe him before.

"Very sexy. And a whole host of other words I'm not going to list right now because the more I talk about it, the more I think about it. Since thinking leads to wanting to *do* it, I'm changing the subject."

They had reached the bridge while they bantered. The walkways were all clear of snow, so he could keep all his attention on Anya instead of where he was walking. He waited for her to say something more, but she stayed silent. Her mouth hardened and her gaze was focused on something in the distance.

"What is it?"

"Not a what. A who and a why. As in what the *fraxx* is *he* doing poking around my bar?"

He looked ahead and knew immediately what the problem was. Yardan, the head of the prince's security force, was having an animated discussion with another male he recognized as N'tev, one of Anya's staff.

"Let's go ask him." He took a firmer grip on his *mahaya's* hand and quickened his pace. Anya broke into a trot, moving fast enough he had to lengthen his stride to keep up.

"Something I can help you with?" Anya asked as soon as they were in earshot.

Both males turned to look at them. Her chef had a relieved expression while the other scowled in annoyance.

Not that it meant much. Damos had never seen the prince's spymaster look any other way. He'd probably renounced his personality at the same time he gave up his last name and a chance at a normal life.

"There's a problem," Yardan said, his gruff voice a perfect match for his stormy demeanor.

"Of course there is. You wouldn't be here if there wasn't. Now, explain what has your wings in a twist and we'll proceed from there." Anya's tone was perfectly pleasant, but the edge of frost in her words would have made even the prince himself reconsider his approach.

Yardan chose to fly headlong into the storm. "I'm going to need the name of every employee you have. Species. Address. How long they've worked for you."

"You already have that. I know because I filed the paperwork myself. Now, what's this really about?" she asked.

"Threat assessment," the spymaster stated flatly.

Anya cocked her head to one side, her lips pursed. "Threat of what? Overindulgence? Random acts of musical entertainment? Spontaneous bot failure? Because if you're here about that last one, I'd love to know if there's some outside force making my droids break down."

Damos had to quell the urge to step in. This was Anya's business, and she could clearly handle Yardan. He wanted to protect her, but he knew her well enough now to be certain she wouldn't appreciate his interference.

Yardan's jaw tightened, a motion that made his short beard seem to bristle. "If you want answers, we need to take this conversation inside."

For the spymaster, that was almost polite.

"Is that your way of asking me if you may enter my club?" Anya nodded to N'tev, who immediately turned and placed a hand on a palm scanner so discreet Damos hadn't noticed it until now.

"Yes." Yardan's gaze landed on Damos. "And I'd prefer that we discuss this in private."

Damos shook his head and let his lips curve into a smile that bordered on a snarl. "Where my *mahaya* goes, I go."

"Your *mahaya*?" Yardan's eyes widened slightly. "Ah. I hadn't heard. Congratulations."

Anya's cheeks heated, but she nodded and then led them all inside.

Damos stayed close to her, his instincts buzzing. Yardan's world was built on information. If he hadn't known about Anya's change in status, something had seriously disrupted the spymaster's focus. Whatever it was, he doubted it would be good news.

Yardan was officious, arrogant, and more set in his ways than a seized engine. She'd met with him several times when she first arrived. Because of her unique circumstances, he'd insisted on multiple meetings to determine if she was some kind of security threat to the princess and her consorts. It was laughable because the princess was probably the biggest threat to security in the known galaxy. Phaedra was a cyber-jockey and a damned good one. She also had no respect for authority, privacy, or intergalactic law.

With Phaedra's "retirement" to Haven, corporations all over the systems had breathed a collective sigh of relief and then quietly increased the bounties on her friend's fuchsia-haired head.

Anya knew how to handle men like him, though. Be firm, don't back down, and be annoyingly open and honest. It made the paranoid ones crazy.

Once they were inside, N'tev went back into the kitchen while the three of them shed their outerwear and then sat at one of the tavern's tables. The air was already thick with the scent of the spiced stew that was today's special, and despite the fact she'd only eaten a little while ago, her mouth watered at the smell.

Yardan seemed to appreciate it too, his expression softening for a moment as he breathed in deeply. "Is that *tarugan*?" he asked.

"It is. Would you like some? It should be just about ready to serve."

And just like that, Yardan's body language changed. His shoulders relaxed and he sat deeper in his chair, one hand rubbing at the close-cropped beard on his chin. "If it wouldn't be inconvenient? It reminds me of another time."

Anya touched the digital menu and input the order, which included three hot chocolates. If food would smooth away some of Yardan's thorns, she'd make sure the male had a steady supply of it.

The droids behind the bar started on the drinks.

N'tev would send out the stew with a bot once it was ready. They were alone.

It was time to talk.

"What's going on?" she asked.

"Some of your recent customers have fallen ill. I'm concerned."

"Are you accusing me of giving my guests food poisoning? That isn't possible." She pressed her hands down on the table and leaned forward. "That kitchen is sterilized every night. The food is fresh and certified."

"It isn't *food* poisoning."

The way he stressed the word *food* sent a chill running through her, like someone had poured a cup of ice water down her back.

"Step carefully, Yardan," Damos said, his voice low and full of threat.

"Yes. Because if you're implying that I poison my customers on purpose, you really shouldn't have ordered the *tarugan*. Who knows what might be in it?"

It wasn't the smartest thing she could say, but she was pissed. Was this male actually implying she'd poison someone on purpose?

"You, no. If I thought that, we'd be having a very different conversation in a much less comfortable location." Yardan gestured around. "But the fact remains that several of your customers are now afflicted with some sort of ailment. I need to know how that happened."

"It's nothing to do with me or my tavern. Killing off

your customers is a terrible business model." She paused and forced herself to drop the verbal attacks in favor of trying to get useful information. "I don't understand how that's even possible. All my customers have nanotech. Hell, the whole damned colony has it except for me and a handful of human colonists who aren't even allowed on this side of the river yet. I thought nanotech was supposed to protect you all from ever getting sick?"

With the impeccable timing that only automated devices could manage, their drinks arrived before Yardan could explain.

Anya took the three drinks off the droid's tray and set them in the middle of the table. "I'm assuming you'd like to choose your own glass?" she asked Yardan.

He shook his head as he pulled out a palm-sized device and ran it over the mugs.

She stared in shock for several seconds. When she next spoke, she had to fight to keep her tone steady. "Did you just scan those *fraxxing* drinks for poison right in front of me?"

If it had been a cold drink, she might have tossed the contents on him, but the last thing she needed was to get in trouble for assaulting the prince's advisor with a scalding fluid. Her life was complicated enough already.

"No. I scanned them for anything out of the ordinary. Nanites, biologicals and the like, not toxins." Yardan took one of the mugs and raised it to his lips, taking a careful swallow of the heated contents. He then set it down with a contented sigh and met her gaze across the table as if he hadn't just insulted her and her bar. "Now that is delicious. Better than anything the food processor I have can make."

Damos grumbled under his breath and took one of the drinks for himself before setting the last one down in front of her. "Now that you've made your point, Yardan, will you explain exactly what the *qarf* is going on?"

"If I knew that, I wouldn't be here asking questions."

Anya wrapped her fingers around her mug but didn't take a drink. "You haven't asked questions, Yardan. You've made vaguely accusing statements and watched my reactions."

Damos managed to muffle his chuckle of amusement in his hot chocolate. It was nice to have him here, quietly supporting her. She could get used to that.

Yardan merely shrugged before saying, "I needed to be sure."

"And are you?" she pressed. She wanted this part over and done with. Head games were tiresome. If something was going on in the colony, she wanted to know what it was and how she could help.

"What I am is worried. Vardarian tech should prevent any of us from getting ill, yet there are multiple cases right now. That has never happened before. Only two things have changed for us. We came to a new planet, and we share that space with a new species. *Yours.*"

"And you think one of us did this? It shouldn't be a long investigation, then. Only a handful of humans are on the planet, and of them, only three live in the main colony. So it's either me, Maggie, or the princess."

"It is not the princess." His tone was sharp enough she could have carved a roast with it.

"Nor is it me. It isn't Maggie, either. She'd die protecting this place and the beings in it."

He inclined his head slightly. "I happen to agree with you about Maggie. Her circumstances are unique, and her companion is still recovering after her capture."

She'd forgotten about Jade. She'd only been rescued a few days ago. Maggie had mentioned that the woman's injuries were healing quickly, but it would take longer for her to recover from the trauma she'd endured.

"So you're here because you're basically out of suspects and you thought you'd see what you could shake loose by coming here?"

Yardan's lips twitched. She couldn't tell if it was in annoyance or amusement. "I'm here because the only thing they all have in common is that they were in this establishment in the last week."

"How many?" she asked.

"Four so far."

Damos asked the next question. "How sick are they? What's wrong?"

"They don't know. Our healers are going through the historical records trying to identify the cause, but they don't need to learn about pathogens to practice medicine because the entire population is supposed to be immune to them all."

That revelation made Anya sit back in her chair. "They don't learn about diseases? At all? Then why isn't there a human doctor on the planet? Not all of us have nanotech. If one of us gets sick, what happens?" She barely paused before answering her own question. "If we get sick, we're *fraxxed*. Tell your healers to contact human doctors. They can help with this. I swear I'm going to kick Phae's ass the next time I see her. That's a hell of an oversight."

The stew arrived, and Yardan dug into it with obvious enjoyment. She noted he didn't bother scanning it before he tucked in. As she suspected, he'd been trying to push her buttons to see what would happen. And if he was coming to her after already clearing her as a security risk, he was grasping at straws. As annoying as the male was, she felt a little sorry for him. He had a monumental task ahead of him, and it would get worse if the illness spread.

"What's being done? What can we do?" she asked once he'd had a moment to eat.

"All ships on the surface are grounded and no one else will be granted permission to land for now. We need to keep whatever this is contained. There aren't any cases on the orbital platform and I'd like to keep it that way."

Anya held her tongue. If something was spreading through the population, it was only a matter of time before it reached the platform. Until today, shuttles traveled back and forth to the station with goods and passengers several times a day. How did this advanced race know so little about how viruses and pathogens worked?

It was a rhetorical question. The answer was obvious. They'd grown complacent and reliant on their technology.

She and Damos continued to ask questions while Yardan ate. His answers were vague and elusive, but she couldn't tell if he was hiding the truth or if he really didn't know. The fact he was telling them anything at all made it clear trouble was coming. She was far from the first person he'd turn to in a crisis.

Yardan dropped the spoon into the empty bowl and stood almost at the same moment. "I have taken up enough of your time. You'll be opening soon. I don't need to tell you not to share what you know with anyone else. The results would be unfortunate. For everyone."

She caught the implied threat and ignored it. If he really had concerns about her, he wouldn't have told her a damned thing. "Of course. Panic and gossip won't help anyone. I will keep my eyes and ears open. If I hear anything of interest, I assume you'd like to know about it?"

He nodded. "I would." He rapped his knuckles on

the table once and then stepped back. "Thank you for the meal. And for your discretion."

"Your trust is an honor," she replied in Vardarian.

The older man's eyes widened in surprise and something that might have been approval. He nodded to her and then turned to Damos and held out his arm to him.

Touching wrists was a common gesture in their culture, usually done scar to scar. She noticed with curiosity that Yardan had no bonding scar on the back of his wrist. That meant he had no *anrik*, which was almost unheard of. She'd have to ask Damos about that later.

They walked Yardan out and secured the door behind him. Only then did Anya let herself relax. This had been a relatively pleasant interaction, but he was not an easy male to deal with at the best of times. Today she wasn't at her best. She was inflamed by the *sharhal* and distracted by pheromones, Damos' well-muscled body, and trying to come to terms with her new reality. Not necessarily in that order.

Damos drew her into his arms and kissed the crown of her hair. "You are remarkable. I have never seen that male so deftly handled. If I ever find myself downwind of his ire, I will ask you to intervene."

She wrapped her arms around her mate's waist and nuzzled his chest. "It wasn't me. It was the *tarugan*. We've found his weakness."

"You believe what you like. I know it was you."

His praise was like being bathed in sunlight, warm

and uplifting. She allowed herself a moment to bask in it.

She was still wrapped around Damos when the kitchen door opened and her staff appeared. All three of them looked concerned and uneasy.

"What did he really want?" Antas asked. He had an arm around Saral's shoulders and she was leaning into his side, arms akimbo as if she was chilled.

Anya just raised a brow. "Don't try to pretend you weren't listening."

Saral laughed softly. "I told you she'd know."

N'tev frowned at her. "You need to sit down, *mahaya*."

Anya pushed out of Damos' arms and took a good look at Saral. Her golden color was washed out and her expression was pinched. "Yes. Sit. Are you okay?" Worry spiked and then morphed into fear. Was Saral sick? Did she have what the others did? Yardan hadn't said much about symptoms. She wasn't even sure he knew the words for them, given that none of them had ever had so much as a sniffle.

Saral waved dismissively. "I'm fine. I just tried to do too much today, that's all. I haven't slept well the last few nights." She shot her *mahoyen* an amused glance. "But that was their fault. It's just a headache and a bit of a backache. I'll be fine by morning."

"If you need rest, why are you here? Go home. All three of you. Take care of each other and I don't want to see any of you here until tomorrow. If you need anything, just let me know."

N'tev and Antas both gave her a grateful smile. "Thank you," Antas said.

"I'm fine! You're the one who should be going home to be with your *mahoyen!*" Saral protested, but she was already being led away by her mates.

"The food. I need to..." she tried again.

"I'll handle it. You're on enforced leave for today. Go. And if you feel any worse, you call the healers," Anya told her.

"We'll take care of her," N'tev said.

"I'm not sick. It's only a headache," Saral grumbled.

"I've run a tavern before, you know. I think I can manage it for one night." She made shooing motions until Saral gave up and went with her mates.

Once they were gone, she turned to Damos. "I think our date is off. I could close down for tonight, but I'm worried people want to gather and talk. I'd like to stay open."

"Of course you'll stay open. With our help. Our evening isn't canceled. It will just start later." Damos folded his arms over his chest in that annoying way that meant he'd already made up his mind and was telling her how it was going to be. *Males.*

She took a step backward so it was easier to meet his gaze without craning her neck. "You don't know a thing about running a busy tavern. Not to mention that you and Tra'var have your own work to do. I'll manage. I always do."

"We have no urgent projects at the moment. We'll

help. While we don't know much about mixing drinks, and I can assure you that you don't want Tra'var anywhere near the food preparation, we know how to clean dishes and follow instructions. Let us help."

"I can handle this. I've got the droids, and if things get crazy, I can call Maggie and see if she can work tonight."

Damos didn't move, but his stance shifted and she got the impression he was now firmly rooted to his spot on the floor. "I am not leaving. You need help, and if the afternoon is quiet, there will be time for you to show me what you need done. If not, you can call Maggie tonight. I want to be here for you. Why won't you let me?"

She wanted to bristle and push back because that's what she always did. Instead, she admitted the truth. "Because if I start letting people help me, I'll get used to it. Then when they take off, I'm disappointed. It's easier not to rely on anyone else."

"You rely on your staff," he pointed out softly.

"I *pay* them."

"They're your friends."

That was true. "They are. But I..."

"I know. You've had time to get to know them. To trust them. Believe me. I understand. But if you don't let us in, how are you going to get to know us? I'm an expert at keeping everyone at a distance. I'm probably better at it than you are." He held out his hand to her. "So are you going to join me out here on this ledge?"

There was only one answer to that question, and

her heart shouted it so loudly it drowned out her doubts. "Yes." She took his hand and held on to it tightly. "Now what?"

"First, you should probably show me the kitchen. Then I need to talk to Tra'var and tell him what's going on."

"You're really willing to wash dishes?"

He tugged her into his arms and kissed her, his lips soft and warm against hers. "I'm willing to do whatever it takes to earn your trust. I know I'm not what you expected, Anya. But I want to find a way to be what you need."

She melted into his kiss. She didn't have the words to tell him what it meant, and she was afraid to say anything in case the universe took note and threw another wrench in her already-mangled plans. So she kissed him back. Her fingers tangled in his vest as she pulled herself up to meet his mouth, and her lips parted on a soft moan. It was as close as she dared to come to saying yes... for now.

10

WORKING with Anya revealed more truths about their *mahaya* than Tra'var believed possible. Her intelligence showed in the choices she made, and the more he learned about why things were done a certain way, the more he came to respect her business acumen. It also made him realize how little thought he and Damos put into that side of things. They could spend hours designing and creating their product, but once that was done, they tended to toss it into the display area and move on to the next project.

Anya seemed to be everywhere at once. She greeted guests when she could, supervised the kitchen area to make sure he and Damos didn't screw up anything too badly, and generally managed to keep everything on the organized side of chaos. They plated the stew and other items not created by the food dispensers, gathered orders, and handed them off to the bots that scuttled in and out. Every few minutes Striker would appear with more used dishes. He and Maggie had both come in to help. Maggie was behind the bar and Striker was doing multiple jobs while keeping an eye on the customers to make sure everyone behaved.

Anya insisted that neither Tra'var nor Damos leave the kitchen. She didn't want either of them being exposed to whatever was making some Vardarians sick. She'd insisted on sterilizing the kitchen before work started and had extra filtration running in all areas of the tavern. "Whatever this is, I don't want anyone else catching it. Especially the two of you."

Tra'var appreciated the sentiment, but he didn't think it was likely he'd catch anything. Whatever was going on seemed to only be affecting a tiny fraction of the population. The healers would figure out the illness, and the specialists would work out why the nanotech wasn't functioning correctly. This would all be over soon. The ancestors hadn't brought the three of them together only to disrupt their lives so soon.

He was grateful for the chance to work alongside Anya, though. It let him see a side of her he might not have seen for months otherwise. She wasn't anything like the female he'd imagined, but the more he got to know her, the more he saw why the ancestors had sent her to them. She wasn't what he wanted. She was what they *needed*, and by all the winds that blew, she was magnificent.

As the evening passed, the orders for food slowed

and the two of them switched to cleanup. Anya came by more often to help as the crowd dwindled.

By the time they were done and the doors were closed behind the last customer, Tra'var was actually fatigued, a feeling he rarely experienced because of his nanotech.

Anya reappeared at the kitchen door, looking as bright and fresh as if she hadn't been working nearly nonstop for hours. "How do you do that?" Tra'var asked her as he dropped the cleaning rag he'd been using into the laundry chute at the back of the kitchen.

"Do what?" Anya asked.

"You have no nanotech or any other enhancements. So how is it you aren't exhausted right now?" he asked.

"Practice. I've been doing this for years. Decades, actually."

Damos shook his head. "And this is what it's like for you every night?"

"Actually tonight was relatively quiet. It's usually busier, and on nights I have entertainment it's a capacity crowd." She gave them both a wide smile. "Even as quiet as it was, it was far easier for me because you were both helping. It means a lot that you were here. Thank you so much."

"You don't have to thank us," Tra'var said.

"But you are welcome," Damos added.

"And I hope you can return the favor soon," Tra'var added.

Anya laughed. "I don't think I can be any help to

you in your work. I have no idea how to forge anything."

"That's not what we need help with. Seeing how you run things here, I think we both realize we're not doing enough to manage our business."

"You mean like the fact your showroom is full of weaponry and the jewelry is all crammed in a dark corner?"

Damos scowled. "It's not that dark."

"I didn't see any prices listed, either," she continued.

"Our customers like to negotiate their own price or trade for goods and services."

She gave them a look of dawning horror. "You don't have set prices? Anywhere? How do you know what it cost to make something in time and materials if you don't have a price? You have a room stuffed full of inventory. You cannot possibly have all that information memorized."

"We have a good idea what everything is worth," Tra'var said, but even as the words left his mouth, he had a sinking feeling she was right. They needed her even more than he thought.

"We can get started as soon as we're done here. I just need to grab a shower and we can go to your place.

"No," both of them said at the same time.

"You helped me. Now I can help you."

"Not tonight," Damos said.

"Tonight we have something else in mind," Tra'var added. The sooner they got her home, the sooner they could claim their stubborn little female and give her the nanotech they carried. Even if there was a chance it wasn't working as it should, it was still more protection than she had right now. It would safeguard her from whatever pathogens this planet had and give her the strength and endurance to keep up with her new mates as they entered the peak of the *sharhal*.

Damos retrieved her bag from the cupboard where Maggie had stashed it earlier. "You're all packed, so now we go home. You can shower there."

"With us," Tra'var added.

"Who? How?" Anya looked at her bag and then at the closed kitchen door and answered her own question. "Maggie. My own staff are conspiring against me."

"Only because you're too stubborn for your own good," Striker called out from the other room.

"I should have never hired a damned cyborg," Anya muttered, but she smiled as she said it.

"Go already!" Maggie yelled. "We'll lock up when we're done."

"Has everyone forgotten I'm in charge here?"

There was nothing but laughter from the other room. "Apparently I'm being tossed out of my own tavern."

"Thank you," Tra'var called out.

"We're taking her home now." Damos held out his free hand to her.

She took it and then reached for Tra'var. The moment their fingers touched was explosive. Energy and need flowed through him like he had hold of a live wire.

"Home. Now," he said.

"Right now," Damos agreed.

"Yes," Anya agreed, her voice lower and husky with desire.

He met Damos' gaze over the top of their *mahaya's* head. His *anrik* nodded once and then smiled down at Anya.

It was time.

It was a good thing Tra'var had thought to order one of the community transports for the journey home. It wasn't a long walk, but now the moment was here Damos could think of nothing else. Need flared over every nerve ending, triggering dark desires so primal he barely recognized them as his own.

It was also snowing, the air so full of flakes they could barely see the road. Fortunately the transport was self-piloting and navigated by sensors embedded in the road. None of them were fit to drive right now, so they rode in silence, all of them holding hands but no one trying anything more. They were all too close to their breaking point.

The moment they were out of the transport, he and Tra'var unfolded their wings. "Go with Tra'v. I'll be right behind you."

It took no time at all for them to reach the rooftop

of their home. His wings were weak, but he could still manage to fly short distances even if he wasn't as graceful as a pure-blooded Vardarian in flight.

They hurried inside, eager to be out of the wind and snow. The moment Tra'var reached the bottom of the stairs he had Anya in his arms, stripping her out of her cloak without bothering with his own.

Damos took a few seconds to shed the first layers of his clothing before joining them, eager to get his hands, and his mouth, on Anya.

His claws extended and for once he didn't hide them. He used them to tear away her clothing, shredding the fabric while still holding on to enough control not to leave so much as a mark on her beautiful skin.

"What is it with you two and your need to ruin my clothes?" Anya asked as the tattered remains of her shirt fell to the floor.

"And you gave me grief for using a knife earlier. Now do you see my point about easy access?" Tra'var asked, his voice slightly muffled as he laid a path of kisses from Anya's shoulder to her ear.

"Yes. Please tell me you ignored my previous ramblings and bought our *mahaya* every beautiful, easily unfastened thing in the shops." He dropped to his knees in front of her, a position that placed her bare breasts within easy reach of his mouth.

"I did. If you want to thank me, just say you'll do the dishes for the next week."

"Done." Damos managed to force the word out of

his suddenly dry throat. Anya was beautiful. Her skin was kissed with a hint of gold and dusted with constellations of tiny spots.

"What are they? Markings?" he asked, brushing a finger over the tops of her breasts.

"We call them freckles," Anya said.

"Pretty. I like them." He let his hand trail lower until his thumb was brushing over one pert nipple. "You are stunning, *mahaya*. Do you taste as good as you look?"

He replaced his thumb with his lips, drawing the already tight peak into the heat of his mouth. Fire streaked through him as she moaned softly, her hands coming up to tangle in his hair and draw him closer.

"Shower. We should get cleaned up before..." her sentence ended with another moan as Tra'var turned her head and sealed her mouth with a kiss.

Damos gave her breast a light nip before moving to the other one. He didn't want to stop. Not when the bed was only a few steps away.

Tra'var had been busy this afternoon. He'd brought the bedding from both their rooms into the main living space, converting it into a bedroom of sorts with a bed more than big enough for the three of them. It would be so easy to tumble her onto the mattress and let the *sharhal* take them...

No. Having a choice mattered too much to Anya to do that. If she wished to bathe first, that's what they'd do, and they'd make sure she had the most memorable shower of her life.

He relayed his ideas to Tra'var through their link, and it only took a few seconds to make a plan.

"Shower is this way," Tra'var gave their mate one last kiss and then led her down the hall. Damos took just long enough to shed the rest of his clothes before joining them.

Tra'var must have directed the in-house AI to activate the shower when they arrived because the moment the door opened all three of them were enveloped in a warm cloud of fragrant steam.

"You had the shower running all this time?" Anya's hair was still braided for work, and now she was coiling the long braid into a knot at the top of her head. Without the curtain of her hair, he could see the long lines of her body—a slender neck, the elegant curve of her back, and the plump roundness of her ass. She was perfect.

"This is not a ship, or a station, little flower. This place is rich in natural resources, including fresh water," Damos reminded her.

"I know, but it's hard to shake some habits, and conserving water is—was—a major concern in my life."

Tra'var turned her toward him and smiled so broadly Damos could have counted his teeth. "It's time to let go of your old life and embrace your new one. Fresh water. Open skies..."

Damos stepped in behind her, capturing her soft body between theirs. "Us."

"Let's start with that last one, please."

Her soft words sent all the blood left in his brain

surging straight to his cock. She wasn't merely making a request. She was granting them permission.

They moved into the shower together, skin to skin every step of the way. The space was more than big enough for all three of them, a design feature he'd never truly appreciated until now. It was meant to give them room to extend their wings while bathing, but it also allowed all three of them to shower together.

Heated water sluiced over them, the mundane act of cleaning up made erotic because of Anya's presence. Soft skin slick with water and flushed from the heat, she was achingly beautiful, perfect, and soon... she would be his.

He wanted to learn every line and curve of her body, every place that gave her pleasure. He turned her toward him and then drew a finger across her lips. One day he'd find a way to capture her beauty in metal. He didn't know what form it would take yet, but he had to do it. Then, even if she retreated from him later, he'd still have a piece of her to worship.

Nails raked across his chest with just enough pressure to sting. "Stop it," Anya said.

No. She couldn't do this to him so soon. She wouldn't... "Stop what? Needing you?" He ground out the words between gritted teeth.

"Oh no. Please don't stop that bit." She flashed him a soft, knowing smile and reached up to smooth a gentle finger between his brows, drawing his attention to the fact he was scowling. "Stop listening to whatever voice is in your head right now, telling you this is too good to last."

"How did you know?" He didn't try to deny it. There was no point. This female saw through him in ways that intrigued and terrified him.

"Because I'm hearing the same voices." She moved her hand so she could lightly tap his temple. "And I'm ignoring them. I don't know what the future holds for us." She reached back to take Tra'var's hand. "But I've finally accepted that whatever else happens, there will be an *us*."

He caught her hand gently in his, drawing it down to his mouth so he could suckle on each finger in turn, his gaze never leaving hers. Then he pressed an open-mouthed kiss to her palm.

"I think what my silent and broody *anrik* is trying to say is that he appreciates your words and would very much like to take you to bed now but he's lost the ability to form words at the moment." Tra'var smirked at him. "Or something like that."

He flicked up the fingers of one hand in an obscene gesture, making sure to do it hard enough the spray struck Tra'var in the face.

"Get the cleanser. Will you? I have something I need to do."

"So that's how this is going to be? First you leave me to secure the forge, and now I'm supposed to fetch the cleanser?"

He brushed his lips to Anya's and winked at her

before lifting his head to look at Tra'var. "As you have so often pointed out. I am the higher-ranking male."

"I've been telling you that for more than half your life and you chose *now* to decide I'm right?" Tra'var managed to grumble and grin at the same time.

"I've always been a bit of a late bloomer."

Anya's delighted laughter bounced off the tiled walls of the shower. "You two are adorable when you bicker."

"I'm adorable. Damos is a grumpy lump of lead." Tra'var filled his hands with cleanser and then handed the container to Damos. Both of them lathered it into a rich, fragrant foam before turning their full attention back to Anya.

"Top to bottom or side by side?" Tra'var asked aloud.

"Side by side I think," Damos replied.

"If this is about what I think it is? I vote for side by side."

"Our *mahaya* has spoken." Tra'var moved a few steps one way and Damos moved the other, keeping Anya between them. Each claimed a shoulder and began spreading the cleanser over her skin, matching each other's movements as they worked their way slowly down to her fingertips.

They repeated their ministrations for each body part as she did the same for them. It was exquisite torture for all of them, the most perfect pain he'd ever experienced.

By the time they reached the apex of her thighs

their movements were no longer slow or gentle. They coaxed her legs apart, both of them wrapping an arm around her back to keep her steady as they slid their fingers into the sweet, slick heat of her pussy.

It was messy, chaotic, and the most erotic experience of his life. They worked in tandem, Tra'var fucking her with his fingers while Damos focused on her clit. He had to be careful to keep his claws away from her delicate flesh. He didn't want to hurt her. Could never hurt her. Anya seemed to know this because she rode their fingers hard, trusting them with her pleasure as she bucked and gasped between them.

His cock was hard enough he could have used it as a forging hammer and he wanted nothing more in the worlds than to bury himself balls-deep in her body. Every cell of his being demanded that he claim Anya. Bite her. Mark her as his inside and out.

"*Soon,*" Tra'var subvocalized to him. "*She needs our protection. Our nanotech. She's too vulnerable.*"

Those words echoed in his head as Anya came apart in their arms. She cried out as her orgasm tore through her, clinging to both of them for support as her knees buckled.

He bent down and gathered her into his arms, kneeling on the floor of the shower as Tra'var drew out the last of her release with his fingers. He bowed his head, using it to shield her from the fall of water as she gasped and trembled in his arms.

She was perfect, beautiful, and theirs to protect.

He knew what he needed to do to keep her safe… but she wasn't going to like it.

Anya almost never relinquished control of anything. Not until she came to Haven. Now she was lying boneless in the arms of her lovers while the small part of her brain that could still form coherent words was suggesting she hand over the running of her tavern to her staff for a few days.

Days.

Crazier still, the rest of her thought that was the best idea ever.

"Pheromones are weird," she announced out of the blue.

Both males chuckled and the next thing she knew she was out of the shower and draped against Damos' chest while Tra'var dried her with a warm, fluffy towel.

"Pheromones are only part of it," Damos told her. "Your body has been reacting to us since the moment we met, and ours has been reacting to you, preparing for this moment."

She raised a hand to touch his cheek. "So, if we're all prepared, why aren't we in bed already?"

"Because Damos is the slowest damned male on the planet." Tra'var gave his *anrik* a light shove. "Do as our *mahaya* says."

She hadn't really looked around the last time they'd been in the main living area. She'd been too focused on her mates to register anything else. This time, she saw what they'd done. The floor was almost completely covered in bedding materials. Mattresses, pillows, sheets and blankets had been gathered to make one oversized bed.

"I guess that answers the question about whose bed we're using."

"You will have your own room eventually, and if you wish to sleep alone, you can. But it's our hope that you will want to spend most nights together with us," Tra'var said.

Damos carried her to the far edge of the bed and then turned so his back was against the wall. He lowered them both to the mattress, adjusting her limbs so they were face to face with her straddling his thighs. His golden skin was still wet from the shower with droplets of water beading on his scales.

He was stunning, like a statue of living gold sculpted by a master of his craft. His thighs were so thick with muscle her knees didn't reach the mattress, a potential issue that was quickly rectified by Tra'var and several pillows. She let them arrange things the way they wanted them, even her.

Both of them stole kisses and caresses, keeping her distracted and adding fuel to the fire that burned in her veins. It didn't matter that she'd come only a few minutes ago. She needed them again.

Tra'var knelt beside them, knees spread, his cock fisted in one massive hand. He was close enough to touch, so she did, leaning over just enough to place her hand on the wide crown of his cock. He let his eyes fall partially closed and groaned as she stroked him with her fingertips, circling the flared head and passing her thumb over the slit at the tip. His hand moved to cover hers, guiding her down his shaft and showing her how he liked it best.

While she gave Tra'var what he needed, Damos took what he craved. He steadied her with one hand on her hip, his mouth trailing fire as he kissed his way down to her breasts.

She rocked in his lap, the heavy bar of his cock a steady pressure against the seam of her pussy. She draped her free arm over Damos' shoulder, letting her fingers tangle in the wet locks of his hair as he tormented her breasts with his wicked mouth.

Damos reached between them, gently parting her folds with his fingers and easing himself into position to claim her.

He was so careful not to catch her with his claws it took longer than she wanted. "Hurry," she whispered and then slid her hand down his back. She followed his spine down to the point where it intersected his wings, exploring the raised ridge of his scales. He growled, his cock growing impossibly thicker.

"If you don't stop that..." he trailed off and gave her clit a warning flick with a callused fingertip.

"Then you'll what? Fuck me slower than you already are?" She threw her words down like a challenge, eager to see the big male's control finally break.

Tra'var uttered a bark of laughter that ended in a low groan as she tightened her grip on his shaft, her other hand still deliberately stroking the spot between Damos' wings.

He snarled something unintelligible and surged upward, giving her what she craved. His newly freed hand landed on her hip, his grip firm and the tips of his claws pricking at her skin. He didn't stop until he was fully sheathed inside her body, her inner walls rippling around his cock.

This was what she wanted. "Yes!"

Tra'var moved closer, his hand over hers as she pleasured him. She kissed Damos and then him, trusting her lovers to keep her balanced as she dove into a sea of carnal pleasures.

Damos' tongue tangled with hers, hot and demanding, consuming her and branding her at the same time. He lifted her into the air and then brought her down on his cock as he thrust upward. She moaned and closed her eyes, her hand moving to his shoulder to brace herself. He dominated and controlled her, dictating the pace of their lovemaking and leaving her with nothing to do but enjoy the ride.

Tra'var's hips bucked, thrusting his cock into her hand faster and faster yet somehow managing to match his pace to Damos'.

She fought to make the moment last, not wanting to lose the magic, the sense of connection to these two incredible males who had somehow become hers. She could blame the *sharhal* or her lust-fogged mind, but she was certain it was more than that. This was right. She knew it the same way she'd known she had to accept Phaedra's invitation to set up shop in Haven.

Damos took her to the edge of her control and then pushed her past it, dropping his mouth to the side of her neck as the first surge of her release tore through her.

She clamped down hard on his cock as Tra'var leaned in and bit her at the point her neck and shoulder met. She felt a moment of pain that was almost immediately swept away by a tidal wave of pleasure.

Damos came next, his cock thickening yet again, increasing the pressure to all her most sensitive places at once. She cried out in surprise and delight as her orgasm intensified, and then Tra'var's seed was scalding her hand as he spent himself against her fingers.

As she slumped against the sweat-slicked expanse of Damos' chest, she smiled to herself. For better or worse, they were now bound to each other—from this day and for the rest of their lives.

That thought didn't scare her anymore.

11

―――――

HER NEW LIFE as a mated woman started off in the most unexpected way. She woke up and discovered it was still dark outside. Normally this meant she'd woken because of some sort of alarm or dire emergency.

Concerned as to why she was awake, she tried to rise only to discover she was partially pinned down by her two sleeping bedmates.

At least, they had been sleeping until she'd woken them.

"What is it?" Damos asked, his voice still thick with sleep.

A handful of dim lights came on as the house's AI detected voices, allowing her to see better.

"I'm awake. I'm never awake this early unless something is on fire." She wriggled free of their embrace and sat up, trying to determine why in the name of gravity she was awake before dawn. Worse. She was wide awake, the kind of mental clarity that didn't usually kick in until she'd had her second mug of tea.

"Only thing on fire is me. Too hot." Tra'var threw off the blankets, giving her a stunning view of his naked body even though the lighting was too dim to make out many details.

Snuggling with the two of them had kept her warm enough that the air of the room felt cool on her bare skin, but maybe Vardarians ran hotter than humans. That would explain his comment. "You two are just naturally hot. Sleeping with the two of you means I'll never be cold again."

Damos grinned at her, looking more relaxed than she'd ever seen him. "We will see to your every need, *mahaya*."

Tra'var grunted in agreement but didn't move. She left their makeshift bed and padded to the sanitation room but only got halfway before she noticed that the usual stiffness and aches weren't so noticeable. That was odd because hours of sex with her two lovers should have had the opposite effect.

Was this the nanotech at work?

She did her business and went to wash her hands and face. Her reflection showed a woman who had been well-loved. Her hair was a mess and her lips were still puffy from all the kissing she'd done. Despite the long day and late night, she didn't have more than a trace of dark shadows under her eyes. The nanotech had to be responsible.

Curious, she brushed her hair back to look at the marks on her neck. Tra'var's had mostly healed, leaving a scar they had assured her would last the rest of her life to mark her as their mate. It was still a little bruised and sensitive to the touch, but in another day or so it wouldn't bother her anymore. Then she turned her head to look at Damos' mark.

There wasn't one.

The skin of her throat was smooth on that side. No scar and only the slightest hint of tenderness. All the joy drained out of her, replaced with a sense of dread. Something was wrong. Why hadn't his claim taken? What did it mean? Was she only mated to one of them? She had struggled to accept this mating. Had finally come to terms with it. She'd embraced it, even. And now... She touched Tra'var's mark again and then the spot Damos had bitten her. She ran back through the events of last night in her mind. He *had* bitten her. She'd felt it.

So much had been going on, and she'd been nearly out of her mind with the *sharhal* and the pleasure of being with them both it was difficult to recollect clearly. Damos had bitten her as she'd come, sending her into an orgasm so intense that even the memory made her shiver with remembered pleasure.

Then Tra'var had claimed her, sending her even more out of control. That bite had stung a little, but the pain had blended with her pleasure and she'd forgotten about it until now. Damos' bite hadn't felt the same.

She turned on her heel and stormed back to the main room. Both her males were still in bed, but she didn't feel like joining them anymore. Now she wanted answers.

She pointed at Damos and then at the unmarked side of her neck. "You didn't claim me."

His smile faded. "I didn't claim you *yet*."

His hairsplitting defense just infuriated her further. "What does that mean? Are we mates or not? I trusted you, and you tricked me into thinking I'd been claimed by both of you."

Tra'var lifted his head to glare at Damos. "You *bakaffa*. You didn't claim her? Why the *fraxx* not?"

"Because my nanotech is inferior to yours," Damos shot back. "So much so that your parents insisted on a clause stating that the blood-bonding ceremony had to be done with purified blood."

"What? No!" Tra'var started to sit up but then fell back onto the mattress with a low groan.

Damos kept talking. It was as if he couldn't stop himself. "You and I are *anrik*. I carry some of your nanotech, but you have none of mine. This way Anya is protected by your more advanced nanotech. It's her best chance."

Anya flew between them to crouch at Tra'var's side. The moment she touched him she knew why he'd been complaining about the heat. He was burning up.

"Lights on! Damos, I'm still mad as hell but we

have a bigger problem." She stroked Tra'var's shoulder. "He's ill. We need to talk to the healers."

"I'm not sick. I'm just dizzy because it's too hot in here."

Damos was already scrambling to his feet. "It's not hot. In fact, it's cold enough my balls are threatening to retreat into my body in search of warmth." He leaned down, scooped up a blanket, and then tossed it over her shoulders. "Too cold for you to be naked. Explain to me why he thinks it's warm?"

"Because he has a fever." She caught Damos by the hand and tugged him over so he could touch Tra'var's shoulder.

"What causes that?"

"Infection. You really have no idea. Do you?" She shook her head. "I can't imagine living such a blessed life that you don't know what a fever is."

Now that the lights were brighter, she could see that Tra'var was showing more symptoms than just his temperature. His eyes were bloodshot and his silver skin had turned a dull gray color.

"Tra'v. What else are you feeling? You said you were dizzy?"

"Little bit." He'd stopped arguing with her, which was both a relief and a cause for concern.

"What else? Sore throat? Can you breathe through your nose? Do you have a headache?"

He blinked at her blearily. "Throat's fine. I'm thirsty, though." He took a deep breath in through his nose and out through his mouth. "Breathing is good.

I'm just tired and hot." His brow crinkled. "And now you mention it, my head hurts. Back, too. Like I went a few rounds at the practice arena and my nanotech hasn't had time to repair the damage."

She nodded and then turned to glower at Damos. "Are you sick?"

"No. I'm fine. I don't understand why he's ill and I'm not."

She didn't get it either, but right now she was just happy at least one of her Vardarian lovers was healthy—even if it was the one she was furious with.

"You need to call the healers and find out what we can do for him. Do they want to see him here or should we go there? While you do that, I'm going to make him comfortable and then call Saral. She was tired and aching yesterday, too."

She'd nursed enough friends, coworkers and crewmates through various ailments to know what to do. She dressed quickly and then went to the kitchen to grab a glass of water from the kitchen. She brought it to Tra'var and set it down beside him. She put two of the blankets back over him, ignoring his grumpy protests about being too hot already. Then she returned to the kitchen and tore through the cupboards until she found some towels and a bowl. She filled the bowl with cold water, added some ice cubes, and returned to kneel beside her patient.

He had managed to prop himself up against some pillows and was drinking the water she'd left for him. "Is that ice?"

"It is."

"Why is it in the bowl and not in my glass?" he gave her a wary look. "What's the ice for, Anya?"

"To lower your body temperature. I can't give you any medication because I have no idea what would work, and I'm not taking any chances." She held his gaze as she deliberately placed the cloths into the bowl and then extracted one, wringing it out without looking at it.

"This is how humans treat their sick?" He set down the glass and glowered. "No."

"I have bad news for you. The patient doesn't get a say in this. Your only job is to do what you're told and get better."

He folded his arms across his chest and shook his head. "No ice."

"Fine." She placed the chilled cloth on his chest. "This is just water."

He cursed loudly in his own language. The words came too fast for her to make out more than a few snippets questioning her parentage, her sanity, and something she was very certain wasn't anatomically possible for either species.

"It's not that cold. It only feels that way because you're overheated."

"I'm overheated because it's warm in here and you've piled half the blankets we own on top of me."

She left the first cloth spread out over his chest and withdrew another from the bowl. She twisted it and then folded it into a square and placed it on his forehead, ignoring his protesting glare.

"Trust me. This will help."

"You're covering me in cold, wet cloths. If this is the human medicine I've heard so much about, I'm amazed your species has survived this long."

Anya bowed her head to kiss him, but he stopped her with a gentle hand. "You shouldn't kiss me. In fact, you shouldn't be anywhere near me. I thought giving you our nanotech would protect you, but now..."

"I'm happy you did it. At least one of my *mahoyen* knows what they want."

She glanced to where Damos stood at the far end of the room, still talking to the healers. His hair was mussed from sleep, but his brows were creased into a deep frown. He was worried.

So was she.

What if the mating bite had been the moment of infection for Tra'var? What if she was a carrier of whatever this was and didn't know it? Had Damos' decision saved him from sharing his *anrik's* condition? *Fraxx. Fraxx. Fraxx.*

"I didn't know that about our bonding ceremony. He's never mentioned it and I wasn't allowed to see the contract." Tra'var grimaced. "He isn't rejecting you. He thinks he's protecting you."

"He's also rejecting himself. I thought we were past this."

Tra'v chuckled weakly and looked at her in bemusement. "I've been trying to get him past this for decades. You are amazing, little flower, but not even you can bring him around so quickly."

"I can try. Or I will once I stop being mad at him for being so *fraxxing* stubborn. And for tricking me into thinking he'd claimed me and then not telling me before I figured it out for myself."

She switched out the now-tepid cloths with ones fresh from the ice water, not bothering to squeeze these out as much.

Tra'v hissed as they hit his skin. "I'm not the one you're mad at. Remember?"

"Sorry. I'm just worried. And pissed."

He caught her hand and squeezed it. "I know. And I like that you're worried about me, even if you are trying to give me frostbite and drown me at the same time."

"Just be glad this planet doesn't have leeches, or I'd demonstrate some really old-fashioned medicine." Her mother had a passion for strange trivia about human history, especially the weird and icky stuff. Her bedtime stories had been dark, fascinating, and fueled more than a few nightmares.

"I'm not even going to ask. I don't want to know."

"Good choice."

Damos finished his call and walked back to the makeshift bed. "I couldn't speak to the healers, but the AI was programmed with all the information they had. I've been instructed to bring him to the main practice arena. They're setting up there to handle all the cases coming in."

"They're expecting that many?" She tried to keep the alarm out of her voice, but the arena was huge. If there were enough cases to justify turning it into a treatment center, things were escalating quickly.

"I think they *have* that many. Whatever this is, it's spreading fast. And no, they have no idea what it is yet." Damos looked down at Tra'var. "But I did confirm that cold compresses are a valid and recommended treatment. Apparently if your fever gets worse, you get to stand in a lukewarm shower."

The look of horror on her mate's face made her burst out laughing. "Make sure you get better so it doesn't come to that." She squeezed his hand and then let it go to push herself to her feet. "I need to check in on Saral and her family. I don't want any of them coming to work today. I'm closing down the tavern for a few days." She took a few steps and then turned to look back at Damos. "I need to be here to take care of my mate." If she was the cause of his infection, it was too late to protect him, anyway. Veth, after last night, it might be too late to protect either one of them. All she could do now was take care of the beings she cared about... and warn her mother not to come back here until it was safe.

Guilt, worry, and regret were warring with each other in Damos' gut. He thought he'd done the right thing by making sure Anya got only Tra'var's nanotech. It had made sense at the time, but he should have told her instead of leaving her to discover it for herself. His only defense was that the *sharhal* had stolen most of his mind and clouded what was left of his judgment.

And now his *anrik* was sick. If Tra'var's nanotech was compromised, Anya wasn't as protected as they'd hoped. He stiffened as he realized what that meant. Anya couldn't be here. She was putting herself at risk.

Anya returned while he was still mulling over the problem. Her jaw was tight and her lips pressed into a grim line. "They have it too. All three of them, though Antas and N'tev only have the first symptoms. They're taking Saral to the arena now."

She moved to return to Tra'var's side, but Damos caught her by the arm. "You can't be near him. I should have thought of that before. You could get sick."

She tugged herself free and glared up at him, anger sharpening her features. "He's my mate. I'm not leaving him." After a painfully long pause, she added. "Or you."

"You have to. I may have been wrong to deny you my nanotech. I'm not sick. I haven't been feeling the cold or getting tired or any of the other things the others are experiencing." He was tempted to offer to bite her now, but he suspected that would only compound his error.

"You didn't just deny me your damned nanotech. You pretended to claim me but didn't. Do you understand how that feels?" Her voice didn't rise in volume but grew more intense, every word carrying an almost physical weight. Or maybe that was just the guilt he felt. He knew what it felt like to be rejected, yet he'd done the same thing to Anya. In hindsight, he wished he'd done things differently.

"I planned to tell you this morning. To explain. But then I forgot and you figured it out on your own." He reached for her, but she backed away. "I'm sorry, *mahaya*."

"Sorry don't feed the bulldog. And no, I don't know what that means, so don't ask."

The pain and distrust in Anya's eyes left him feeling like someone had opened his chest and poured molten metal inside, but he wouldn't regret what he'd done to protect her. Tra'var wasn't flawed like he was. He wanted only the best for Anya, even if it meant denying his own desires... and hers.

"You need to go home. If you need anything, call me, but don't leave. You have to protect yourself."

"No. I'm going with you."

"You can't." He held up a hand to forestall her next argument. "It's not my rule. Until they know what this is and where it's coming from, only Vardarians are allowed into the arena. It should contain the spread. At least that's what the instructions said."

Her expression grew so stormy he half expected tiny bolts of lightning to appear around her head. "Yardan. That male needs to have his paranoia surgically removed. When is he going to realize we're all in this together? Why is he even involved? This should be Tyran's decision and there's no way he'd do this."

"Did you just refer to the prince by his first name?"

"Well, yeah. That's how he was introduced to me. I'll work on my courtly manners another time. Right now, I need to talk to Phaedra and find out what the *fraxx* is going on."

Knowing his *mahaya* was friends with the royal family who had founded this colony was one thing. Listening to her announce her intent to call them up and demand answers was something else again. It was also something of a relief to have her anger focused somewhere else. It would return to him eventually, but maybe by then he'd have some idea how to fix this.

Maybe.

An ice cube arced through the air between them. "If you two are done posturing and snapping, I've got a few things to say."

"You should be resting," Anya told Tra'var.

"Bit hard to do when the two beings who matter the most to me are having a fight not five steps away from me," Tra'var pointed out as he traded the cloth on his forehead for a cold one from the bowl.

Anya's lips curved up in a ghost of a smile. "Compresses are working?"

"They aren't not working. That's all I'm saying about it."

They all laughed, and for a tiny sliver of time, everything was as it should be. The three of them were caught up in a moment of shared laughter, free of anger, worry, or hurt.

Then Tra'var shivered and paled, his color fading to a flat gray. He threw off the compress and huddled deeper into the blankets.

"Human medicine sucks va-vacuum. Now I'm f-freezing," he said, teeth chattering.

Anya swore. "You've got the chills. It's part of the fever cycle. We really need to get him to a healer."

"*I* need to get him there. You need to go home," Damos said.

"Hey, still talking h-here." Tra'var waved weakly, his hand barely outside the blankets. "Damos, you're a *bakaffa* for what you did."

"Yeah, a total bastard," Anya agreed.

Tra'var shook his head. "I wasn't finished. Anya, I know you're angry and hurt, but he's still right. You need to go. The longer you're with me, the more likely you are to get sick."

"This isn't how it's supposed to be. We're mates. I should be with you no matter what."

"Not if it means putting yourself at risk. We won't let you do that," Damos said softly.

Anya made a sound of strangled frustration and threw up her hands. "I'm going to stop arguing about it because it's a moot point. Tra'var needs to see a healer and I'm forbidden to set foot inside the arena. I'll speak to Phaedra, find out what the *fraxx* is going on, and get that order changed." She pointed a finger at each of them.

"And when that happens, I will march to wherever you are and refuse to leave because that is what mates do."

A dozen arguments sprang to mind, but Damos kept his mouth shut. As persuasive and stubborn as she was, he highly doubted Anya could make the prince or Yardan change their minds. If it gave her something else to focus on and kept her safe at the same time, he'd consider it a victory.

"I'm not thrilled at being separated from you either, *sandar*, but Damos will take care of me. He's got no choice. If something happens to me, he'd have to spend more time with the customers and handle the books himself."

"Alright, I'm going. *For now*. Call me when you're settled in at the arena." Then she turned to him. "Take care of him, Damos." She raised her hand and then dropped it without reaching for him. "And take care of yourself, too."

She left, and Damos took a moment to make sure she hadn't taken her things with her. Relief hit him when he saw her bag full of personal items still in its place. Their newly lit flame might not be burning brightly right now, but the embers were still there. He'd find a way to rekindle that fire... but not until he got Tra'var to the healers.

He bundled his *anrik* in every blanket he could find, ignoring his half-hearted protests. He called for a transport and then lifted Tra'var into his arms and made for the stairs they almost never used. It was usually quicker to step out onto the balcony or the rooftop and fly.

"So this is what it feels like to get carried around?" Tra'var commented. "Maybe we should look into a decent flight harness for Anya. This is not nearly as comfortable as I imagined."

"Anya weighs about as much as two feathers and a pebble compared to you," Damos retorted. "Have you considered going on a diet?"

"This is all muscle, thank you." Tra'var's jesting tone turned serious. "If this doesn't turn out well for me, I need you to promise me something."

"We are not having this discussion."

"Yes, we are. I'm the sick one here, so you have to humor me."

Damos scowled at him. He really didn't want to talk about a future that didn't include his best friend. "You know I'll take care of her."

"I know. I want you to promise me you'll let her take care of *you*."

He didn't know how to answer that, so he didn't.

"Promise me."

"Forge and fire, are all sick people this stubborn and cantankerous?"

"Based on my extremely limited experience, yes. But you're not sick so what's your excuse?"

They reached the door to the outside and Damos set his *anrik* back on his feet, making sure not to let go until he was sure he wouldn't fall over. He'd never seen Tra'var look like this. Pale. Weak. Uncertain.

"I'll let her take care of me. But it's not going to come to that. You're sick, not dying. If this was serious, you wouldn't have the strength to argue and complain. The scientists will figure out how to fix the nanotech, the humans will help us treat this pathogen, and the three of us will celebrate this mating properly."

An empty transport rolled up outside. The road was already marked by the passage of other vehicles despite the fact it was barely dawn. The colony was already awake this morning, and all the tracks led the in same direction—to the arena.

A cold, unpleasant feeling slithered down Damos' spine and wound itself into a tight ball in his gut. If this many were sick already, how long would it be before no one was left to take care of the stricken?

At least Anya was as safe as they could make her. Locked away in her home with plenty of food and drink, she could stay secluded for however long this crisis lasted.

12

———

IT WAS A CLEAR, chilly but beautiful morning. Anya watched dawn chase the darkness from the sky, filling the world with light and color once more. Not that there was much color to be seen. Everything was blanketed in a fresh fall of snow. Her boots crunched as she walked, her stride shortened to make sure she didn't lose her footing. The roads hadn't been cleared yet, which meant she could see the tracks of vehicles imbedded in the snowy surface. A great many tracks, which was odd. The Vardarians flew most of the time, and when they weren't airborne, they preferred to walk. So where was everyone going so early in the morning?

The answer became obvious when a vehicle passed her. Of the three occupants, two of them were bundled in blankets as a third sat across from them, grim faced and worried.

They had to be sick, just like Tra'var.

Yardan's words of yesterday came back to her as clearly as if he was standing beside her. *Some of your recent customers have fallen ill.*

Could this be her fault? Had some freighter crew come to her tavern and inadvertently infected her or one of the staff? That didn't explain why the Vardarians' nanotech was malfunctioning, though. If that was the case, why did she feel energized after a long and very vigorous night of lovemaking? She should have been asleep for hours yet.

There were too many questions she didn't have answers to. She needed more information before she reached out to Phaedra and demanded to know why Tyran was breaking the most fundamental rule of the colony he'd established. They should be facing this problem as a united community.

She reached an intersection and paused. If she continued straight, she'd be home in a matter of minutes. The nearest medical building was a few blocks to her left.

She turned left. If she wanted answers, that was the best place to start.

The clinic was eerily quiet. Her instincts told her there wasn't another living being in the place. It made sense that it would be empty, but it was still a strange feeling.

"Hello?" she called, feeling slightly foolish. If an AI was around, it would already know she was here.

"Hello. What can I assist you with?" a female voice

spoke and the air in front of her shimmered and then coalesced into a hologram of a silver-skinned Vardarian female.

"Uh. Hi. I'd like to get tested to see if I'm carrying any pathogens or anything that might cause problems for my Vardarian mates. You can do that. Right?"

"Scans and bloodwork would establish if you had any current infections or other health issues. If you will follow me, we can continue this consultation in an exam room away from other patients."

She was alone in a room talking to a hologram. No one was around to eavesdrop, but the AI's protocols were hard coded. "That would be fine."

The hologram led her to a small area off the waiting room with several identical doors, which she assumed led to other exam rooms. Most of the minor functions were handled by the medical AI and droids. The healers' focus was emergency treatment for accidents and serious injuries... until now. She imagined that every healer in the colony was currently getting a crash course on infectious diseases and how to treat them.

The room was almost identical to every other one of its type she'd ever been in. Pale walls, a small counter space, a narrow bed and a few chairs. The medical droid sat in standby mode in one corner, its various limbs folded against its frame.

She was directed to stand in a corner with a small circle on the floor. The scans were done in less than a minute, though the holographic attendant informed her that the results couldn't be released until they'd been reviewed by a healer.

"Are you aware that your pregnancy inhibitor has expired?" the AI asked as Anya removed her heavy cloak and rolled up her sleeve in preparation for having blood drawn.

The question surprised her. "I wasn't. It must have slipped my mind. Can you inject a new one while I'm here?"

"Unfortunately that item is not currently in my inventory. A shipment is expected in ten to sixteen days. Do you wish to be notified when it's in stock?"

"Please." There wasn't a snowball's chance in a supernova she was going to get pregnant at her age, but between Tra'var's sudden illness and Damos' lie of omission, she wasn't ready to take that chance. Even if part of her wasn't as opposed to the idea as she tried to pretend. Until a few days ago, she'd expected to live her entire life alone. Things were changing quickly. Who knew what the future might bring?

She answered a few more questions and asked a few of her own while the droid took samples. The AI didn't have any new information about the strange illness, but that wasn't a surprise. She couldn't imagine the healers or the council would update an AI before sharing the information with the general populace.

That thought had her digging in her pocket for her comms. Why *hadn't* there been an official announcement yet?

"Am I done?"

"Yes. Your results will be sent to you once they've been compiled and reviewed. I cannot give you an estimate on when that will be due to the current situation."

"Can you tell me if I have any obvious indications of infection?"

The hologram gave her a conspiratorial look so realistic it was uncanny. "The scans showed nothing that would cause me to recommend that you seek further medical attention."

"Thank you." Anya rose, donned her cloak, and was already checking the community feed for updates as she followed the hologram back into the waiting area. Once there, the image raised a hand in farewell and then faded away.

She might not have all the answers, but at least she knew she wasn't sick. Whatever Tra'var had, the odds were good she hadn't been the one to give it to him.

One worry gone. Several dozen to go.

A community-wide update *had* been issued while she was getting scanned. It didn't tell her anything she didn't already know, but not everyone had been questioned and then updated by the prince's spymaster about the matter. Now, everyone was aware of the problem and had a list of symptoms to reference. The posting also made it clear that the humans and cyborgs were to use caution and refrain from any contact with their Vardarian neighbors. It was infuriating, and the wording of the whole thing made it clear that the prince hadn't written it. This had to be from Yardan.

She started to type out a quick text message but then changed her mind and sent a ping requesting an audio call when Phaedra had a moment.

Her comm chimed before she could put it away, the tone an indication she had an incoming voice message.

"Hey, Phae. Thanks for getting back to me. I need to ask—" was all she managed to say before Phaedra interrupted.

"Anya! Where are you? How are you? Do you know what's going on? Wait, of course you do. Otherwise you wouldn't be calling me at the crack of dawn. Also, I'd be furious with you for not telling me you're mated but things have been a little chaotic so I will be mad at you later."

Anya blinked at her comms. "Have you been drinking *ja'kreesh*?"

"Yes. Can you tell? No, wait, don't answer that until you answer my other questions." Without video, it was harder to read her friend, but the brittleness to her words was worrying. More was going on with Phaedra than just an overdose of Torski-brewed rocket fuel.

"I'm fine and on my way to the tavern." Anya had to swallow hard before she could add. "Tra'var is sick. Damos took him to get help, but I can't go because your asshole *mahoyen* banned humans from the site. What the *fraxx* is that about?"

"It wasn't Tyran. He..." Phaedra's voice cracked and then she shifted to the trade language the translators didn't recognize. "Tyran and Braxon are both sick. They're being treated at home. The council is doing their best, but Yardan is convinced this is some kind of attack. I can't say any more than that right now."

"Can you come to the tavern? It's shut down until this craziness is over," she asked in the same language.

"I..." Phae sighed. "I don't want to leave them, but the truth is I can't do much here. Plus I could use a break. They're both difficult patients, who are not coping well with their current reality."

Anya snorted. "Yeah. Tra'v was the same way. Apparently never being sick a day in their lives has left them woefully unprepared for this." It felt good to be talking to Phaedra about this. She couldn't be the only one feeling this way, either.

She switched back to Galactic Standard. "Come to the tavern. I'll make us some hot chocolate and see what desserts are left over from last night. And for the love of gravity, don't tell Yardan where you're going. I've seen enough of him already."

"I'm on my way. Wait. When did you see Yardan?"

Anya had to stop and think for a moment. Had it really only been yesterday? It felt like so much longer. "He dropped by yesterday to poke around and insinuate that I or one of my staff had something to do with all this."

Phaedra demonstrated just how many languages she knew by cursing in all of them without taking a breath. "I wasn't informed he'd done that."

"It's fine. I fed him and he turned into someone almost pleasant for a while. Meet you at the tavern? I'm ten minutes away."

"See you there. It might take me a bit longer to slip away without anyone noticing I'm gone. With everything going on, they're treating me like I was made of glass."

"But so far no humans have got this, whatever it is, and you have medi-bots as well as Vardarian nanotech. You should be fine."

It took Phaedra just a half-second too long to reply. "You know what Yardan is like. He's paranoid on a good day, and this is not a good day."

More was going on than Phaedra was admitting. That was fine with Anya. She could keep her secrets. Right until she set foot in the Bar None. Then Anya was getting to the bottom of things.

Anya had enough time to make two mugs of cocoa, top them with whipped cream, and set out a platter of leftover desserts with a few fruit tarts, a couple of brownies, and a stack of Maggie's trademark cookies. "Breakfast of champions," she declared as she took a seat and helped herself to a cookie.

She was on her second one when she heard footsteps on the porch. "Come on in, Phae. I left it unlocked."

The door opened as Phaedra called out, "I'm sorry, Anya. This was not my idea!"

Then Yardan marched inside with Phaedra trailing after him.

Anya got to her feet. "You weren't invited, Yardan. And we're out of *tarugan*. No reason for you to be here. Shoo."

"He caught me slipping out the back. When Tyran is out of bed, he and I are having an overdue discussion about what happens when people try to control my life." Phaedra shot a withering look at Yardan.

The spymaster glared right back at her. "You wanted to go out. You're out. You insisted you didn't need your security detail, so they are not here. With the prince and his *anrik*... unavailable, your protection falls to me."

"The hell it does," Phaedra said over her shoulder as she marched past him to give Anya a rib-cracking hug.

"Hi. Congrats on your mating. Sorry your mates are sick. Hello, brownies! Now this is a proper breakfast." Phaedra let go of her to pick up a brownie and then dropped into an empty chair.

Yardan hadn't moved.

"Oh for the love of... Why are you here? She's fine. I'm not going to poison my friend. If you're so worried about Phae's safety, you can stand outside and guard the door."

Phaedra sighed. "He's still here because he's afraid something will happen to the prince's heir."

Yardan stiffened. "You are not supposed to speak of it yet! And brownies are hardly something a female in your condition should be eating."

Ah. That explained a few things. "You're pregnant? Congratulations! How far along?"

Phaedra beamed. "A little over two months. We're not saying anything yet since it's still early."

"And you're healthy?"

"As a horse. Yardan is just being paranoid."

"That's my job," he replied.

Anya gave in. She kicked out another chair and nodded to it. "If you're staying, sit down. Order yourself something to drink if you want."

"Thank you." She didn't wait for him to sit before turning her attention back to Phaedra. "Why are the humans being kept away from the sick? We didn't do this. None of us have any signs of infection."

"It's safer this way," Yardan said before Phaedra could speak.

"For who? Have you thought this through, Yardan? What happens if this bug keeps spreading through your species? Who will take care of the sick when *everyone* is sick?"

"I asked him the same thing," Phaedra chimed in. "Apparently Vardarians aren't good at asking for help. Like, at all."

"But that's already happened. I mean, the healers here have contacted some of the other species for help to figure this out. Right?"

"We have," Yardan said.

"I reached out to my friend Alison. She's a doctor out on the Drift with a lot of experience treating humans and cyborgs. She and her husbands are still on what's left of Astek Station, taking care of the remaining residents until the new station is ready. Anyway, she's got people working on it, but we don't want word of this getting out, either. We have to be careful."

That caught her off guard. "Why?"

"Because someone or something has weakened the Vardarians' nanotech. That's never happened before, so it's not likely to be random chance. We can't let whoever it is know it worked," Phaedra said, her voice solemn.

"*Fraxx.*" With everything going on, she hadn't had time to consider what a nanotech problem really represented.

Anya mulled that over for a moment and then looked at Yardan. "All the more reason we need to pull together right now. If this community has been attacked, we should all be doing what we can to help. Is Denz working on solutions to the nanotech problem? What about some of the cyborgs he's been mentoring?"

"They're already on it. Vixi has taken samples and sent them along, but she and the other healers are all starting to show symptoms. One of her fathers is literally coordinating things from his bed."

More footsteps outside announced they had another visitor. Both women looked up and Yardan got to his feet.

Maggie walked in. "Oh, hey. Was out walking and just sort of wound up here. Sorry for intruding."

Anya waved her inside. "Get in here and grab a seat. Better yet, go make a few more mugs of cocoa and then sit down. Yardan could do with one, too."

The spymaster had sunk back into his chair without saying a word, which was worrying. And was it her imagination or was his golden skin tone looking a little flat and faded?

"On it." Maggie headed for the bar. "So, we talking about this damned bug and the fact that none of us are allowed to help our friends?"

"We are," Anya said.

"Excellent. On behalf of every human colonist stuck on the other side of the river—all of whom have messaged me already today—this is bullshit. This is our home too. And don't get me started on the cyborgs. They're furious."

Phaedra sighed into her hot chocolate. "I told you."

Yardan nodded the slightest bit. "You were right. If we knew what this was and who was vulnerable then maybe..."

"Nope," Maggie called out. "That's not your decision to make. If I decide I want to take the chance to help my neighbors, that's my call. The council isn't happy about this either. Are they?"

Yardan's shoulders slumped. "They are not."

"But Denz is scrambling to deal with the nanotech issue. Raze is on the other side of the mountains with his family. All the Vardarians on the council are symptomatic. River and Edge are raising hell, but they don't have quorum." Phaedra's lips twisted into a grimace. "We never planned for this."

"Welcome to reality, where no plan survives for long." Maggie set down a mug in front of Yardan and pulled a chair out for herself. "If we're making this up as we go along, is there any reason why the others can't be here?"

Yardan scowled. "No one should be out right now."

Phaedra waved him off. "I think we're past that. In fact, I know we are." She looked at Anya. "How many cookies do you have in the kitchen?"

It was an easy decision. "Enough. Call them, Maggie. We might as well all be together for this."

They sat in a more or less comfortable silence while Maggie called the human colonists. She then programmed in an order for more food and cocoa and returned to the table.

"They'll be here shortly. River is driving them over, which tells you everything you need to know about how eager they are to do something," Maggie reported when she returned.

After taking a sip of her drink Maggie leaned back in her chair and asked, "Does anyone even know what this is, yet?"

"No idea. It could be anything. Tra'var has a fever, body aches, headache, and fatigue. Saral and her mates apparently have the same thing. That's all I know."

"The ones who sickened first have some kind of

skin lesion. It's lifting their scales and causes discomfort," Yardan said.

"It hurts?" Anya asked. "No one said anything about pain."

Yardan set a portable holo-projector on the table and called up a file. "Apparently it doesn't hurt, but it does itch. It first appeared last night."

A medical report appeared on the display. Anya didn't bother reading it.

"What kind of rash? Do you have images?"

Phaedra glared at the spymaster. "If he does, it's news to me."

"You were caring for your *mahoyen* and I didn't want to disturb you. You tried to sneak out before I could inform you of an update."

"You could have told me on the drive down here," Phaedra said between bites of cookie.

"You informed me you weren't speaking to me. I took that to mean you didn't wish me to speak to you either."

It was like being in the middle of a family squabble as the favorite niece tormented the grumpy uncle. Anya cleared her throat. "Ahem. If we could get back to the matter at hand?"

"Of course." Yardan tapped the projector and the file was replaced by several images, each one enlarged enough so they could all see it easily.

Each image was similar. Gold or silver skin had raised and clearly irritated scales.

"Are these all on the torso?" Maggie asked.

"Looks like it." Something was nagging at the back of Anya's mind. Something whispering she'd seen this before, but where? She'd never seen a sick Vardarian in her life. They were apparently as rare as a unicorn's first tooth.

Voices outside announced more guests were arriving.

"Good thing this place doesn't have any speed limits yet or River would have some explaining to do," Phaedra commented.

The relative quiet of the tavern was shattered as a group of human women came through the door. Anya had never met any of them before. Normally they weren't permitted to cross the bridge into the rest of the colony. They were still acclimating to life here and the restrictions ensured they wouldn't find themselves claimed by a pair of Vardarian males before they were ready. Anya hadn't liked the idea of keeping the human women isolated, but now she'd been claimed herself, she could see the logic. She'd been here longer than any of these women and she was still struggling to deal with her new reality.

Maggie introduced them, but Anya only caught the first few names. Nasha, Dani, and Kara. Kara should be on a ship back to Earth by now. She'd decided that life on Liberty wasn't for her. Why was she still here?

"Kara asked to come even though she's not staying," Maggie explained as if reading Anya's mind.

Kara nodded, but her shoulders were tight and shadows lay beneath the young woman's eyes with lines of strain around her mouth. She was obviously unhappy about her departure being delayed. One look and Anya could guess why. Carefully manicured nails, artfully styled black hair with streaks of red that were just starting to fade, and a face perfectly painted with cosmetics despite the early hour and the fact they were all facing a crisis. This woman wasn't built for life in a rural colony.

"I want to help. With the quarantine in place, I can't go anywhere, so I might as well make myself useful," Kara said.

"Grab a chair and a drink. If you need anything, let me know and I'll see what we've got in the kitchen," Maggie said and gestured to several nearby tables.

Dani ignored the food and moved closer to the projection to get a better look at the images. She raised a hand, tracing the pattern of the lesions with her index finger.

That's when Anya realized why it looked so familiar. Spirals of spots. She *had* seen this before. "Is that star pox?" she asked.

"Helix fever." Dani nodded. "Same disease, different name, but that's got to be what it is. I was a medic back on Earth. I've seen this plenty of times."

Phaedra groaned. "I should have remembered that. I'm sorry, Dani. I've been dealing with a lot and I didn't consider you might have insight." Then she perked up. "But if it's just star pox, that's good news!"

Dani looked thoughtfully at the images. "Possibly. But I have no idea how it will react in a new species.

Pherans and Jeskyrans never catch this bug, but it jumps back and forth between humans and Torskis with no trouble. From what I've read, it can knock a Torski on their ass for weeks. In humans it's unpleasant and debilitating for a week or so, but that's about it."

There was a collective sigh of relief from everyone, and then Phaedra burst out laughing. She laughed until tears rolled down her face and everyone watched her with concern as she wiped her eyes, tried to speak, and then broke into another round of sniggering giggles.

It was relief as much as amusement, Anya knew. She felt the same way. Tra'var wasn't going to die from this, and she couldn't have given it to him because she had been vaccinated against that ailment. So had every human here. It was part of the standard package everyone got if they spent any time traveling in space because the virus was as contagious as it was annoying.

"Princess?" Yardan finally spoke. "I don't understand what you find so funny."

Phaedra managed to compose herself enough to answer. "Of all the things in the galaxy it could be, it's only star pox. I thought—but it's nothing! Well, almost nothing. I've had it, and it sucked, but the way your people have been reacting you'd think half of them were on death's door."

Dani cocked her head in confusion and then started to laugh. "Now I get it. They've never been sick before, so now they've all got the Vardarian version of the man-flu."

"Man-flu? I thought you said it was called star pox or helix fever. How many names does this accursed ailment have?" Yardan scowled at them in annoyed confusion.

"Man-flu is a human term for... you know what, let's not get into that right now," Phaedra said with a smile. "The good news is that with this bug, serious illness is rare. Unless this is something wildly different, everyone should recover and be none the worse for the experience."

After that, the conversation derailed for a few minutes while everyone chattered, sharing what they knew about treatments and cures.

Phaedra let it continue for a time and then raised her voice to bring everyone back on track. "This is good news. Everyone here is vaccinated against this. Right? If not, raise your hand."

No one did.

"Dani, can you give us a crash course on how to help the sick? We might not be medics, but we can make sure everyone is taken care of." Phaedra looked around the room. "If you do this, you might end up mated by the end of the day. If you're not ready for that, you're welcome to walk home or come with me to help me with my mates and any staff who fall ill. They're all claimed, so you would be safe from the *sharhal*."

"I'll go with you," a dark-haired woman said softly. "I love it here, but I'm not ready for that step just yet."

"Okay, Suki is with me. Anyone else?"

The rest shook their heads, even Kara.

Maggie tapped her temple. "I'm relaying this to Striker. He's going to gather up the rest of the cyborgs and meet us at the arena. They're all immune, too, and we could use the help."

"You got the implant? When?" Anya asked.

"While you were busy getting your *sharhal* on." Maggie smirked at her.

The other women turned to gawk at Anya. "You got claimed? What's it like? Who?" The questions flew at her like a meteor swarm.

"I'll answer questions on the ride to the arena. Phae, you should get back to your males. I can help here and we'll keep in contact. You and Yardan have some new updates to post to the colony."

Phaedra nodded and rose. "We do. And thank you, everyone. *This* is what Haven is supposed to be—a community looking after each other."

A round of cheers went up loudly enough no one heard Skye come in. The cyborg's grim expression softened as she saw the hope on everyone's face. "Does this mean we have a plan?"

Yardan got to his feet but then lost his balance and made a grab for the table. He missed and hit the floor on his knees.

Phaedra gasped and rushed over. "You stubborn *fraxxing*, idiot. You didn't tell me you were sick, too."

He growled. "Not sick. Just got up too fast."

Skye walked over and extended her hand to the fallen spymaster. He took it and tried to get to his feet.

Skye shook her head and bodily lifted him off the floor, draping his arm over her shoulders and grabbing him around the waist. "I got you."

Yardan grunted. "Apparently. Damned females shouldn't be that strong. And I'm fine."

"Don't let go of him, Skye. He's not close to fine. Can you help me get him home?" Phaedra asked.

"Sure thing. You can fill me in on what's happening on the way."

Suki went to gather their coats and joined them at the door.

"I'll send you a summary of what you need to do and what to watch out for. It's basic stuff," Dani said.

Anya took a deep breath and smiled a little. The future looked brighter than it had an hour ago. They still had challenges to face and a lot of work to do, but she wasn't afraid of hard work.

Now there was hope, she could admit the only thing she'd been afraid of was losing was her chance to spend the rest of her life with Damos and Tra'var.

A new truth dawned brighter than the sun outside. Somewhere in the middle of the craziest time in her life, she'd gone and fallen in love. As usual, her timing was spectacular.

13

———

Tra'var dozed off on the short ride to the arena. He dreamed a little, but when something startled him awake all he could recall was that his dreams had been as vivid as they were disturbing.

He opened his eyes, hoping Damos hadn't caught his moment of weakness. It was a foolish hope. His *anrik* sat across from him, a shadow of worry in his amber eyes that vanished once he saw Tra'var was awake.

"Enjoy your nap?"

"I was just resting my eyes," Tra'var retorted.

"Of course. I forgot that when you close your eyes it shuts off your hearing too. That explains why you haven't answered any of my questions in the last five minutes."

"Anya said I'm supposed to rest."

"So now you're taking her advice? You weren't too keen on it when she was dousing you in ice water."

"Keywords being ice and water. And instead of coming to my aid you announced it was a good idea. Medically sound. I'm going to remember that."

The vehicle turned and Tra'var stopped talking as a wave of dizziness hit.

"We're nearly there," Damos said. "Want me to open a window?"

"*Fraxx* no. I'm cold enough as it is. If this is what humans endure every time they get sick, I am more than grateful I was born with nanotech. This is miserable."

Once they arrived, Tra'var got out on his own, but he knew within a few steps he didn't have the energy to make it inside without assistance.

Damos didn't say a word, just offered him a supporting arm and helped him inside. The place was almost unrecognizable. The sand was gone, and the maintenance bots were now scuttling back and forth with makeshift trays affixed to their upper surfaces so they could carry supplies and other items.

Inside the area proper were scores of beings, some seated on the ground and others lying in simple prefabricated cots. The arena was the largest communal space, so it made sense to make it the emergency shelter. It was standard practice in the empire, but he'd never seen one active before.

"Now, I'm worried," Damos said softly.

"Me too." But he still had faith—not only in their

ancestors but in this community and the beings who lived here. They'd find a way through this.

A silver-skinned Vardarian female approached and greeted them with a weary smile. "I'm Healer Vixi A'Nir. Please come with me. We're waiting for more cots to be produced but we can get you settled on chairs. Can you describe how you're feeling? Hot? Cold? Tired?"

He leaned into Damos and let his *anrik* do the talking.

"I'm Damos and this is Tra'var. Our mate is human. She says he has a fever, dizziness, headache, body aches, and fatigue. Currently he is experiencing what she called fever chills."

Vixi nodded. "Thank you. That tells me exactly what I need to know. You said he has these symptoms. What about you?"

"I am normal. Nothing has changed for me."

Tra'var might be sick, but he was still alert enough to see the healer's surprised reaction.

"Nothing? Not even fatigue? We've determined that all of our people are experiencing some level of nanotech failure."

He felt Damos tense before speaking again. "I'm not pure Vardarian. My mother was an unmated female with both Vardarian and Ferrym blood. I was never given the usual genetic treatments."

The healer nodded, a glint of what might have been hope in her eyes. "Ferrym? Of course! Similar but with enough variances..." She trailed off and then smiled. "I need you to come with me."

"I can't. I have to see to my *anrik*. Our *mahaya* isn't permitted to help and there's no one else."

Vixi nodded, and for a moment her professional mask dropped and Tra'var saw the female was exhausted. "You're sick too?" he asked.

"We all are, or we will be soon." She looked intently at Damos. "Everyone but you. I need to find out why that is before we're all too sick to do anything about it."

"What can I do?" Damos asked.

Tra'var used up the rest of his energy to clap his friend on the back. "I think she's saying you might be the answer to this whole mess."

Damos looked utterly stunned. "I am?"

The healer nodded. "Your genetics, yes. You're immune. We're not. And your nanotech appears to be working perfectly. Thank the ancestors, you might be the key to unlocking this puzzle."

A droid moved past them, hauling a small trailer stacked with cots ready for setup. The healer snatched one as they went by and handed it to Damos. "See to your *anrik*. I'll be back to fetch you in a few minutes."

"Right."

If he had the energy, Tra'var would have laughed at the expression on Damos' face. "Ha! The ancestors have done it to us again. Now get that set up for me and go save the colony. And I never want to hear you say another word about your inferior anything. Unless we're talking about your cooking. I still say I'm better at it than you are."

Damos shot him a lopsided grin. "You need to lie down. You're clearly delusional."

Within minutes he was stretched out on the cot, wrapped in his own blankets, and wishing he could do more to help.

"Don't forget to update Anya. You're in enough trouble with her already."

"I won't. Now shut up and rest or I'll go find some ice and a bucket."

Tra'var didn't bother to answer that. He just made a rude gesture and closed his eyes. He trusted the ancestors, his *anrik*, and his *mahaya* to sort things out on their own.

Damos had never been so thoroughly examined in his life. He'd been scanned, scraped, and poked with needles while being asked a dizzying number of questions by a variety of healers and others who didn't introduce themselves. They were all clearly unwell and he saw several of them drinking *ja'kreesh*. Normally the beverage wouldn't do much since the nanotech they carried gave them better endurance than any substance could. It also removed anything harmful, which mitigated most of the effect anyway. Only now, with their tech failing they had turned to the same techniques the humans used to stay alert long after they'd reached their physical limits.

It explained why Anya's system had responded to even Tra'var's weakened nanobots. What would she be like once things returned to normal? He grinned a little. They might need an update just to keep up.

Everyone was doing their best, but he'd seen Anya in action. If she were here, she'd have things organized and streamlined while still managing to make everyone feel welcome.

He missed her already. She was right. She should be here. Tra'var needed her. *He* needed her.

He sent her a brief text message, trying not to overthink his words. Then he sent it quickly before he could change his mind.

Tra'var is settled. I'm doing what I can to help. I'm sorry for what I did last night and I wish you were here with us. One day I hope you can forgive me.

D.

He checked on Tra'var first. The male was dozing comfortably, which was good. He'd heard any number of patients be told the best thing they could do was lie still and rest. He felt for the ones still well enough to take care of the others. They couldn't rest, not when so many were in need of tending. Couples and families stayed together with parents caring for their children and trying to hide their worry from the little ones. He couldn't imagine what they must be feeling right now. Unlike his mother, these parents loved their children and would do anything to protect them, but they couldn't really do anything to defend against a virus they should all be immune to by default. If he were a father... *qarf.* He'd be going out of his mind at a moment like this.

The thought of fathering a child didn't give him the same sense of unease it always had before. In fact he could almost imagine what that could be like. A child with Anya's hair and amber eyes just like... his. A sudden ache filled him. A need he'd never known before. It had to be another side effect of the *sharhal.* If the child had his eyes, they'd carry his genetics, too. They'd be flawed, just like him.

That thought didn't feel right to him. Not anymore. Now wasn't the time to think about it, though. He had work to do and neighbors to help. Anya had been right about that, too. This was a community, and right now it was struggling. Keeping the humans and cyborgs away was foolish.

Like many of these buildings, the layout of the arena was standardized. It took him no time at all to track down the emergency supply rooms. Some were full of specialized equipment that wouldn't be needed, but they also held plenty of bedding and other items to be distributed. He found the servo-droid command center and took over from the sick and weary male trying to organize things.

He programmed new instructions and brought the rest of the fleet into active service. Normally the bots and droids ran in shifts with half of them recharging at any time. Today they needed all of them. If Vixi was right, this arena would soon be full of sick, worried beings. He didn't want to think about what it might look like if they couldn't figure out what this illness was or how to stop it.

He also didn't want to worry too much about why Anya hadn't responded to his message yet. She was obviously still upset, but he wanted to know how she was doing.

Instead, he pushed his worries aside and tried to focus on the here and now. If they made it through this, he'd fix the mess he'd made and then claim her the way he should have the first time. He'd thought they would have time, but this *fraxxing* illness and the demands of the *sharhal* weren't going to give it to them. For now, he had work to do. He left the control room and moved on to the next task... feeding everyone.

He wasn't the first to think of it. A makeshift kitchen had been erected in the designated area, and food dispensers were producing orders of simple broth and other light meals already.

"I can load a cart and start handing these out," he offered to the group and was met with grateful smiles and nods.

A female stepped forward with a welcoming smile. "You're well enough? Oh that would be wonderful. Every round we make someone gets too tired to continue. I'm Irisa, and I think I'm in charge."

"She is," a familiar voice said. It was N'tev. "But only because she's as bossy as her cousin. Damos, it's good to see at least one of us is still hale and hearty. How's your family?"

"Tra'var is ill, and Anya is furious she isn't allowed to tend him herself. How's Saral?"

"Stubborn enough to try and insist she can still help," Irisa muttered. "I sent my dear cousin back to bed and told Antas to lie on top of her if she tried to get up again."

"Normally that wouldn't be a good idea. Hopefully he's weak enough he won't—"

"If you finish that sentence I'm going to crawl up to the roof and throw myself off," B'ron said from somewhere behind Damos. "I don't need to know. I don't *want* to know."

"Then you and your *anrik* best move out soon because once we're better, we'll want to celebrate our recovery. Loudly and repeatedly."

B'ron threw his hands in the air. "I just came to see if there's some soup. Kotar is awake and hungry. I want to get something into him before he goes to sleep again. Please don't make me hear anything more about your sex life."

Irisa laughed. "We can talk about mine if you like?"

B'ron just looked at Damos. "Help me."

Damos chuckled and braved the kitchen to grab one of the bowls of broth Irisa had just prepared. "Take this and go. Quickly."

He took the soup. "Thanks. You're my new hero."

Damos waited until the young male was on his way back to his *anrik* before he added, "Just remember you wouldn't exist if your mother hadn't enjoyed getting naked with your fathers."

The male gave a horrified squawk and walked faster, his head down and wings partially expanded as if that might somehow protect him from anything else they might say.

Everyone else laughed and Damos laughed with them. It felt good, and for the first time since he'd arrived, he felt a moment of real connection to the beings he lived with. They were in this together. More than that, they wanted him to be part of things.

As the laughter faded, a different energy settled in the room—one of determination. Everyone stood a little taller as they got back to work. Damos filled one of the carts with bowls of soup and packets of wafers that would provide all the nutrients a body needed. Eating one was like snacking on dehydrated *gharshtu* dung, though, which was why the broth was necessary.

He was on his third round of what they were now calling the "ward," when he heard a disturbance at the main entrance. A growing number of voices and the stomp of feet had him leaving the cart to find out what was happening. So far the arrivals had come in a steady but manageable stream. If all these new arrivals were ill, there'd be no way the few still on their feet could keep up to the demand.

The first figure to appear out of the throng was the one he most wanted to see, and one who shouldn't be anywhere near here. *Anya.*

She made straight for him, her lovely face

wreathed in smiles and giddy excitement. Despite his confusion he managed to brace himself in time to catch her as she flew into his arms at full speed.

"I'm still mad at you," she announced as she kissed him. "But we'll sort that out later."

He kissed her back, the *sharhal* blazing back to life the moment he touched her. "Hello, my *choran*. I have never been happier to see anyone in my life, but... why are you here?"

"Because we know what this is and how to help," she announced, loudly enough her voice carried across the relatively quiet space.

The reaction was immediate. Heads turned, murmured conversations stopped, and everyone stared. For once, being near the center of attention didn't bother him.

"How? What is it?"

A human female he'd never seen before walked in, also beaming. "We call it helix fever, or star pox. It's a common human ailment, but not a serious one. We're working on confirming this diagnosis, but since we're all immune, we're here to help. My name is Dani, and I'm a medic. Where are your healers? I need to speak to them."

A buzz of excitement and hope filled the area as Vixi stood and waved a tired hand. "I'm over here."

Dani blinked. "It's just you?"

"I'm the last one still on my feet," Vixi admitted.

Dani hurried over to her. "Then it's time you sat

down. You rest. I'll talk. The others already know what to do."

The others? Damos turned back toward the entryway. Humans and cyborgs were still arriving as others filed into the ward. Hundreds of them. Thank the ancestors.

"And there's no risk to you?" he asked Anya.

She snuggled in closer to him. "None. I've had this bug as a child, and as an adult I'm vaccinated against it. Now, how's Tra'var?"

"Resting and grumpy."

"So no change then. And you? Are you okay?" she asked, her arms still wrapped around his waist and her head on his chest with her face tipped up so they could talk.

"Now you're here, I'm perfect. And healthy. So much so that the healers have been taking all sorts of samples in hopes they can use my immunity to help the others."

Her mouth quirked up into a half-smile. "And you thought you were protecting me by withholding your mating mark."

"A decision I will regret for the rest of my life." He cradled her close, bowing his head over hers so he could bury his nose in her hair. "We're needed here, but at the moment we aren't..."

"The next words out of your mouth better be a promise to bite me."

"I will mark you as mine, place your *harani* on your arm myself, and then Tra'var and I will ensure you don't wear anything else for several days. Possibly a week."

"And no more leaving me out of things even if it's for my own good?"

"That's not going to happen again. We parted only a short time ago and I've already realized that was a mistake. Though in my defense, it wasn't my doing."

"No, that was Yardan, and he's seen the error of his ways. He's also too sick to interfere anymore, so Phaedra has left me in charge."

"What do you need me to do?"

She gifted him with a smile that sent light into even the darkest corners of his heart. "You just did it."

14

───────

HER NANOTECH MIGHT BE WORKING at minimal levels, but it was enough to give Anya the energy she needed to stay on her feet. She was in constant contact with Phaedra, coordinating their efforts, brainstorming ideas, and sharing their progress. Phaedra was getting regular updates from her friend Dr. Jefferies, and so far it had all been good news.

The energy in the ward had brightened, too. The fear had faded, and everyone was breathing easier now that they believed they wouldn't lose their loved ones to this ailment.

Getting everyone back on their feet would take time, though. Identifying the culprit had only been the first step in what turned out to be a complex process that sounded more like fairy magic and sorcery to her. She left the science and magic to the experts and got on with what she was good at—managing chaos and heading off problems.

A quick scan of the ward didn't indicate any new issues. In fact, things seemed relatively calm. The cyborgs were everywhere, helping the sick, preparing meals, and assisting wherever they could. Dani was cloistered with the healers working on solutions, and the human colonists were taking care of those who had no family to help them. Even Cameron was helping, his flirtatious manner gaining him popularity with all the females, even the mated ones.

A soft sob caught her attention and she scanned the area, looking for the source. It took her a minute and a bit of walking to find it. Kara was hiding in the shadow of one of the outer pillars, her face in her hands and her shoulders shaking with more muffled sobs.

Anya's first reaction was annoyance. Kara wasn't sick. She wasn't even going to stay at the colony. She had no one she cared for among the sick, so why was she crying instead of helping the others?

She brushed aside her irritation quickly, though. The woman hadn't handled any part of her new life very well, so it was no surprise this would overwhelm her. It was frankly surprising she hadn't gone with Phaedra to avoid any chance of meeting her mates. If that happened, she'd have to stay, and that wouldn't end well. Some beings just didn't have the temperament for this kind of life. "What's wrong, Kara?"

The woman flinched, shoulders rounding defensively.

"Whoa. Easy. No one's going to hurt you. And if they did, I'd have my mates beat them senseless and toss them in their forge so you didn't have to see them again." She didn't think that was likely, but it gave her something to say to draw the other woman out.

"They're going to. And I deserve it. I didn't know. They said—" she sniffled and finally lifted her head. Guilt was etched into every line on Kara's face.

Anya moved to face Kara and then squatted in front of her, ignoring the slight protest her knees made at this unexpected abuse. Nanotech or not, her joints had over forty years of mileage on them. She took Kara's hands gently and said, "No one is going to hurt you, Kara. You have my word. Now, what are you talking about?"

"I did this." The woman's blunt confession set Anya back on her heels.

"Did what? What did you do?" She had to work to keep her tone soft and neutral. She wanted to shake Kara by the shoulders and demand answers.

"I did this." She wiped a tear-soaked cheek and then used the same hand to point to the patient-filled arena. "I didn't know. They said it was just an experiment and no one would get hurt. But they had to find a way to weaken the aliens' nanotech. Because... because..." Kara lapsed into sobs again, leaving Anya clutching to the last shreds of her patience.

"You mean the Vardarians. Someone wanted to run an experiment on them and you agreed to help."

Kara nodded, tears dripping off the tip of her nose.

"You released the virus?"

"No. No virus. I wouldn't do that."

Anya's temper surged. "What did you *do*, Kara?"

"They arranged for me to come here. Paid me enough to get my whole family off Earth and to a nice, civilized planet, not just a colony but an established world where we could live like kings."

Bitter bile rose in the back of Anya's throat. This woman had agreed to help someone experiment on the colony so she could buy her way into a better life? "I don't care why you did it. I need to know what you did."

"They sent me here. Told me to blend in and wait for a package to arrive. Then, all I had to do was follow the instructions. They promised no one would get hurt!"

"Who brought you the package?"

"I don't know. I came home from classes one day and a box was sitting by my front door. We did that a lot, dropping off little gifts and treats for each other, so I thought one of the other girls... but it wasn't. There was a cylinder inside. Metal. Small enough to fit in my hand. The instructions were simple. The next time I knew I'd be close to a Vardarian, I was to put the canister in my pocket. When I got within a few meters, I was to push the button on one end. That's it. The moment that was done I could go home."

"How long ago?"

"Six days. I should have been on my way home by now. I swear I didn't know this would happen."

Anya couldn't keep the acid out of her next words. "You didn't think releasing something that would attack the Vardarians' nanotech would do them any harm?"

"They said..."

"Who are they?"

"I don't know. There was a man. Blond. Short hair. Dark suit. His suit was nice. I mean the kind that costs more than most of us make in a year sort of nice. He spoke really well, too. Polished, you know?"

"Did he have an accent. Could you tell where he was from?"

"Uh, I don't know. Proper. He didn't speak like anyone I'd ever met."

Given Kara had never left Earth until coming to Haven, that didn't narrow it down much. "Did he give you a name? Any clue who he worked for?"

"He said his name was Mr. Grayson. Told me what I was doing would protect our kind from the aliens. That we had to take steps to keep our place in the hierarchy."

That did not bode well. Not on any level. "And you believed him."

"We've got to do something! Every alien race we come across is better than us. Stronger or faster or smarter. We're going to end up as slaves or pets."

"We're already slaves to our own corporations. Don't need aliens for that. We did it to ourselves."

Kara just looked at her, but nothing in her expression indicated she understood Anya's point. "So, what happens to me?"

"You've got a lot to answer for."

"But I'll still get to go home. Right? I mean, eventually?"

"That's not up to me." And Anya was sure that whoever made the final decisions wasn't going to let Kara go with a pat on the head and a gentle reminder to be nice to others.

"You need to come with me, now. We're going to go find River and you'll tell her everything you just told me."

"River. I like her. She's nice... for a machine." Clearly Kara had decided that by unburdening herself of the truth she was now free to continue to be honest about everything, including her bias against nonhumans. It wouldn't help her cause, but that wasn't Anya's problem. Her job was to hand over Kara and then get back to fixing the mess the biased bitch had made of her home.

The hours blurred together. She spent time with Tra'var when she could, but each time he drifted off she'd go back to work. She had managed to be there when it was his turn to get the mix of healing accelerant and new nanotech based on Damos' samples. Denz had outdone himself, finishing the new version after the rest of the techs had collapsed from illness and exhaustion. The Vardarians had never lived a day without their nanobots, and they'd all learned a hard lesson about how much they depended on them. Without that protection, their immune systems were almost nonexistent.

Someone had done this to them on purpose. The thought chilled her to the core of her exhausted soul.

She sank down on a stool next to Tra'var sometime before dawn. Damos came and wrapped a blanket around her shoulders before pressing a mug of hot soup into her hands.

"Rest. You've done all you can. The rest is up to him." He kissed her cheek. "He'll want to see you when he wakes up."

"Thank you." She leaned against his leg and smiled up at him. "I'm proud of you."

He blinked at her. Then a slow smile dawned on his face, one that didn't stop until he was grinning down at her, the skin across his cheeks turning a brilliant gold. He was blushing.

"Thank you." He bent down and kissed her tenderly, his lips moving as they brushed hers. "I love you."

He was gone before her tired mind could form an answer, but his words left her filled with a warm, contented glow. Taking Tra'var's hand, she sipped her soup and waited for him to wake.

Tra'var woke from a dream about ice-filled rivers to discover it hadn't all been his imagination. Cold water trickled through his hair to pool at the back of his neck, and something wet and chilly lay on his chest.

He heard a soft splash somewhere nearby and he opened his eyes just in time to see Anya lift another cloth from a bowl of water. He caught her wrist before she could reach him.

"No more ice or I'm going to need treatment for frostbite next."

"You're awake. How are you feeling?" She dropped the cloth to clutch at his hand.

It was the same question she'd asked him the other times he'd woken to find her sitting beside him. This time, his answer was different. "Good." He sat up to demonstrate. The dizziness and fatigue weren't gone, but they'd diminished to the point he barely noticed.

"Your fever broke overnight, and so far there's no sign of the rash appearing. I think you're on the mend."

He pulled the wet cloth off his head and held it up. "If my fever broke, what's with the cold compresses?"

A tiny smile twitched at the corners of her mouth. "If I say it was to make sure it didn't come back, would you believe me?"

"I would have, if you hadn't smiled."

"My poker face suffers when I don't get enough sleep." She shrugged. "I wanted to clean you up a little. I asked Damos to bring me some water. He brought me a bowl of ice water and said it was time you got your ass out of bed."

"And you went along with this plan?" He'd only been out for a day or so and already the rest of his trio were ganging up on him. It was clear that Anya, at least, had pushed herself hard. Her hair had pulled loose of its braid in places, and dark shadows lay beneath her eyes. Whatever endurance his nanotech had given her was long expended and he guessed the booster everyone was getting hadn't kicked in yet.

"Well, he might have also mentioned he still owed you for dropping him in that river."

"I have been betrayed. I am wounded beyond words." He pressed a hand to his chest.

"You are clearly feeling better if you have the energy to be dramatic."

Tra'var stretched, even unfolding his wings enough to loosen more of his muscles. "I am. I have also decided that I will accept this betrayal gracefully if it means the two of you have worked things out."

Anya laughed. "We'll get there. But it's not like we've been sitting around discussing our personal problems while you and most of the others have been waited on hand, foot, and wing."

He took a moment to look around him, the reality of how bad things had gotten finally apparent. His fever and fatigue had left him only vaguely aware of what was going on around him, but now...

Beings milled about everywhere. They lay on beds or sat on stools and benches. Those well enough moved about and helped those still recovering. Cyborgs and humans moved through the sick handing out food and offering aid or just companionship.

Movement on the upper floors caught his attention. Beings moved about up there, too. "Is the entire colony here?"

"More or less. Some of the cyborgs are running the factories and others are working on the new nanotech booster. It's replicating fast enough, but it still has to be prepped and then loaded into the injectors. The sickest got the first doses, and now we're working on getting it to everyone."

"Damos saved us."

"He did, though he's having a little trouble adjusting to that fact. He's become something of a hero. Everyone knows who he is now, and he's finding it all rather bewildering."

"I bet he is. It's good for him, though. Where is he?"

"Last I saw he was with a group of children. Many of them are already fully recovered and have energy to burn, so he took them outside for a snowball fight."

That stunned him. "Damos is playing with children *voluntarily*?"

"He is. Oh, no, make that he was. That must be them coming back now."

A cacophony of chatter and noise heralded the return of a group of snow-covered, grinning children all clustered around Damos. He had two of the smaller ones perched on his shoulders.

"I think my fever is back. I'm hallucinating," Tra'var said.

"You're not." She leaned in to kiss him. "You're going to be fine. We all are." She nuzzled his cheek softly. "I'm glad because it means I get a chance to tell you something."

"What's that?"

"I love you."

His heart took flight and he hauled her into his arms, kissing her hard.

"I love you, too. When I thought I might not make it, I realized losing a life with you would be my greatest regret."

He didn't stop kissing her until Damos joined them. "So the ice water worked?"

"You're a complete *bakaffa*. But yes, I'm awake now."

"About time." Damos fixed Anya with a fierce glare. "He's awake. Now will you please get some rest?"

Tra'var frowned. "How long has she been doing this?"

"Since yesterday." Damos' expression turned grim for a moment. "It's been a long night, especially since our *mahaya* refused to take the booster until every Vardarian had theirs."

"Stubborn female. Why not?"

"Because others needed it more." She looked up at Damos, a shimmer of heat lighting up her eyes. "And I was sort of hoping I could get mine from the source."

"Go. Take our mate home and claim her properly."

Damos snorted. "Say goodbye to Tra'var. If he's well enough to try ordering me around via our link, he can manage on his own for a few hours. I'm taking you home. It's time I rectified my earlier mistake."

Anya made a delighted little squeak and flung herself back into Tra'var's arms. "We won't be long."

A low growl erupted from Damos, throaty and deep. "Oh, I think we will."

He managed to steal a kiss before Damos tugged Anya away. Tra'var had expected them to walk out, but his *anrik* surprised him again by unfurling his wings.

"Hold on," he told Anya and then launched himself into the air, his wings working furiously to gain the lift he needed.

This was why Damos didn't fly often, especially not if anyone but Tra'var could see the effort he needed to take off without a running start. It would seem that didn't matter to him anymore. At least not today.

"Don't forget to deactivate the ice maker or you might wake up dreaming of frozen rivers like I did!" he called out as they rose.

Anya laughed.

He watched until they reached the upper tiers and flew out of the arena. Then he carefully got to his feet. There was still work to be done, and he was well enough to stop being a patient and start helping those who weren't yet recovered.

Damos and Anya needed this time. When he saw

them again, they'd be a true trio, bound by blood for the rest of their lives.

Damos couldn't have flown the full distance home with Anya in his arms, but by some bit of luck or fate, the wind was blowing from the right direction let him glide most of the way.

He hadn't even let Anya get her cloak on before they left, but with her help he managed to fold his around her well enough to keep the worst of the cold at bay.

He landed a short walk from home, but Anya stayed burrowed against his chest and clung tighter when he tried to set her down.

"I'll stay here if you don't mind. I'm warm and comfy right where I am." She peeked up at him. "Please?"

Forge and flames, even if he'd wanted to set her down, he couldn't have done it after that request. If she'd asked him to find her a dragon to ride, he'd have done it. Now that she was back in his arms, the mating fever had returned stronger than ever. He needed her so much he ached with it.

His claws extended, scales tightening across his body as something raw, primal, and pure tore through him. It was more than lust. More than love. It was all-consuming. He ran the rest of the way to the house. No one was around to see him, but for once he didn't care if they did.

Anya was laughing and kissing him, her touch pouring more fuel on the fire already searing him from the inside out.

The shop entrance was nearest and he hurried to it, barely pausing long enough to gain access before they tumbled inside.

He'd intended to apologize, to woo her with sweet words and gentle touches. However, all his good intentions scattered like ash in a whirlwind. He set her on her feet to kiss her properly, giving her only a moment of freedom before he crowded her up against the newly closed door, pinning her in place with his body. He ground himself against her as his mouth slanted across hers. He tore at their clothing with his clawed hands, shredding the fabric until they were both naked save for a few tattered bits of cloth caught between them.

She was nearly as demanding as he was, tearing away the scraps until she could reach bare skin. She raked her nails over his chest and flanks and then tore her mouth from his to kiss the same places she'd scoured.

He had to step away from her to get free of his pants and boots, and when he looked up again, she was naked save for the cloak of her unbound hair. She'd drawn it over her shoulders, falling in unruly waves over her beautiful body.

This was how he wanted to capture her likeness,

soft lines and curves containing so much life and energy that she burned like a star. Once, he'd thought to create a piece of art so he'd still have a piece of her even after she'd turned from him. Now, he knew what a fool he'd been. She was his as much as she was Tra'var's—forever loved by them both.

He drew her into his arms and then let them both sink to the ground, the shredded remains of their clothes becoming their love nest.

"Hurry. The *sharhal*. It burns," Anya whispered the plea against his mouth, her words shattering what little control he had left. Her bond to Tra'var was already forged, but until he claimed her, the mating fever wouldn't relent. Now that the crisis had passed, the full force of their need was all-consuming.

He cupped her breasts, kissing her as his greedy hands stroked, fingers toying with the tight buds of her nipples.

She stretched, parting her thighs in open invitation, and the sweet scent of her arousal filled the air. He drifted one hand lower, skimming down her body to the apex of her thighs. His fingers delved into her folds, the wet heat of her desire making her slick to the touch.

"Damos!" She called out his name as she arched her back, lifting her hips to buck against his hand.

"I know, *choran*. My beloved. But I will not risk hurting you."

She caught his face in her hands, pushing him back until she could look into his eyes. "You will never hurt me. I know that now. You are my *mahoyen*."

"Yes. And you are more than I ever imagined I could have. I love you, Anya. I will love you until my last breath rejoins the eternal wind."

"I love you too. So much it scares me."

He moved to kiss her but she shook her head, her eyes suddenly wide and wild. "Fraxx. I forgot. I went to the medical clinic yesterday to make sure I wasn't the source of Tra'var's infection. During the scan I discovered my pregnancy inhibitor has expired. I still don't think I can get pregnant at my age, but I know you don't want children..."

Love and need flowed together to forge a new kind of madness. He turned to kiss her palm and then smiled down at his beautiful mate. "I may not be as sure of that as I was. Shall we leave it up to the ancestors?"

The smile she gifted him with was like a balm to his soul, healing the last of his scars. "I think we should, but only if you can promise me one thing?"

"Anything."

"Any child we might have, any way we have them, will be free to be who and what they are. No genetic tinkering. I want our home to be a place of acceptance, not compliance with some genetic ideal that would erase part of their parentage."

That put everything in a new perspective for him. Even through the lust that fogged his brain, he couldn't imagine wanting to scrub all traces of this amazing female from their children. "Done."

This time when he tried to kiss her, she slid her

hands around his neck to pull him in even closer. He moved over her, nestling between her thighs and rocking his hips so his cock stroked along the seam of her pussy.

She wrapped one leg around his waist, making it easy for him to seat himself at her entrance. When he paused, she nipped at his lower lip and bucked her hips against him.

"I want to be yours, Damos. Now."

"You *are* mine, Anya. Always." He claimed her as slowly as he could, feeling her body give way to his as he eased himself deeper. He was only halfway home when she flexed her inner walls around his cock, the pleasure of it tearing a groan from his chest.

He surged into her, burying himself to the hilt in her glorious body. He stilled for one heartbeat and then two. Then he let himself go. They came together in a frenzy of need, feverish with wanting. Hot breath, the sting of nails and teeth, the heat grew between them until it felt like he was the one being forged, hammered and shaped into something new.

He fucked her harder as desire coiled like a spring deep in his groin, winding itself tighter with every thrust. They raced each other up a mountain of pleasure, and when they reached the peak, he dropped his mouth to the side of her neck and bit her.

She came apart in his arms as her blood flowed into his mouth, and at the moment of orgasm he nicked his lip with a fang, letting his blood flow into her.

This time, she didn't leave it to him. With a wild

little cry, she bit him back, her teeth breaking the skin of his throat exactly where a Vardarian female would place it.

His senses exploded with a release so powerful it wiped his mind clear of everything but the raw pleasure of this moment, and the satisfaction of knowing she now belonged to him.

Her pussy was still squeezing his cock with random aftershocks when he finally raised his head to look at her. He could taste her blood on his lips as heady as summer wine. "You bit me."

Her eyes gleamed with smug satisfaction, pleasure, and a hint of defiance. "I did. And the moment I get Tra'v alone, I'm biting him, too. I may not be able to mark you properly, but I am laying claim to both of you anyway."

He touched the spot where she'd bitten him. "When I get you upstairs, we'll put some ointment on us both. It will create a scar despite our nanotech."

"You will? It can? So this time your mark will really take?"

"It better. Or I will bite you every day until it does." He eased out of her body to settle at her side.

She rolled over to snuggle into his embrace, the two of them content to hold each other as the *sharhal* faded.

Then, a thought struck him and he chuckled as he contacted Tra'var, not bothering to subvocalize. He wanted Anya to hear this.

"*She's ours now, Tra'v. But for now, I have the*

better claim. She bit me. Hurry up and get better so she can do the same for you."

Anya laughed so hard he nearly missed his *anrik's* reply. "About *qarfing* time."

He had to agree, and in his heart, he silently thanked his ancestors for sending them the perfect female. This time, Tra'var had been right to trust them.

EPILOGUE

THE AIR inside the arena buzzed and thrummed like a living thing. The sickbeds and bedding were gone, replaced by tables laden with food and drink, all of it cooked and carried here by the citizens of Haven. It was the biggest potluck Anya had ever seen, and it was amazing. She sampled everything she could, making notes about spices, seasonings, and ingredients. Tomorrow she'd have to meet with her kitchen staff to determine what they could add to the tavern's menu. Today they were celebrating.

She tasted a new dish, the flavors exploding on her tongue as she bit into what she'd thought was a simple meat pastry. "This is delicious. You have to try some!" she said, holding out her plate to Damos and Tra'var.

"Where are you putting all this food? Do humans have an extra stomach somewhere?" Tra'var waved off the offered plate and then patted his stomach. "I filled up half an hour ago."

"Nanotech has benefits I'd never considered." Like a metabolism that would have made even her teenage self envious. She had the energy of a teenager, too, and the endurance to keep up with her two equally energetic mates. She'd also discovered the advantages of Vardarian clothing. Easy access had never been more important, especially when one of her *mahoyen* had claws that could shred any garment giving him too much trouble.

Life was good, even if storm clouds still lurked on the colony's horizon.

She heard snippets of similar conversations everywhere. Discussions about who might have hired Kara and why they'd done it. Some were uneasy about what would happen when more colonists arrived from Earth next spring. Would more saboteurs mingle in their ranks? Even some of the human females were worried. This was officially their home, too.

Maggie and Striker came over to join them, accompanied by her friend Jade and two big cyborgs who followed Jade around like they were her personal security force. Wreckage and Ruin had been part of the team to rescue Jade and Maggie, and they had taken on the role of her protectors.

"Hey there," Anya waved and held out her plate. "You have got to try these. Jade, how are you liking your new place?"

Jade smiled a little. "It's perfect. Thank you. The

other place was nice, but it was too quiet. I'm not used to that."

"I'm glad you like it. Has Saral stopped sending you meals every two hours whether you want them or not?"

Anya had moved in with her *mahoyen* a few days ago and Maggie had suggested that the apartment above the Bar None might be perfect for Jade. She was now working part time for Anya doing droid and tech maintenance. Jade might have had most of her cyber-jockey tech violently ripped from her body, but she was still a hell of a mechanic. She'd performed some sort of wizardry on the bar-droids, which had worked without a single malfunction since the day they'd reopened.

Jade laughed for the first time since Anya had met her. "I've got her down to once every four hours, plus snacks."

Saral had adopted Jade on sight and had folded the woman into her extended family without hesitation. She'd done the same thing for Cameron, who was thriving under her care and attention.

"Did you hear about Kara? She's been handed over to the military." Maggie shook her head. "Why would Nova Force be investigating an attack against an independent colony?"

Anya didn't know the answer to that question either. "Phae isn't talking and neither is anyone else on the council. There's got to be a reason, but they're playing this one close to their chests for now." She shrugged. "I trust them to make the right call, but I hate that we're not being told everything."

"Me too. I'm not fond of secrets," the former cyber-jockey said.

Anya patted Jade's shoulder. "If it helps? Neither is Phaedra. She wouldn't agree to this if she thought it was detrimental to the colony."

Striker spoke up. "How's the new nanotech working? Everyone seems to be fully recovered."

"Thanks to Damos' contribution, we're all back to one hundred percent. Word has been sent back to the empire warning them that they might want to make some changes, too. Whoever hired Kara to do this isn't likely to stop after one failed attempt," Tra'var said.

"All I did was give samples. Denz, the techs and the healers deserve the credit," Damos demurred.

Anya gave him a playful slap on the arm, right below the *harani* he now wore on his bicep. "You promised not to do that anymore."

He looked down at her with adoration and amusement. "Sorry, *mahaya*."

Jade cocked her head. "With Kara in custody, whoever it is will know their test failed, but they won't know why. That's something at least. Right?"

Anya sighed. "Unfortunately, no. Kara was supposed to leave right after she released whatever was in that canister. The only reason she was still here was because Yardan's rampant paranoia led him to shut down all traffic on and off the planet at the first sign of illness."

Damos nodded. "And the experiment only weakened our nanotech. No one could have known that *fraxxing* idiot freighter captain had falsified his crew's immunization records. He had crew members with helix fever and lied about it, and then he let them go on shore leave."

"Which is why some of my customers were among the first ones to show symptoms. I hope he loses his ship for this." Anya still couldn't believe the captain had done that. It was a violation of one of the key rules of the trade. He'd put an entire colony at risk because he couldn't be bothered to maintain his crew's health.

Jade's expression turned grim. "Son of a bitch. I hadn't thought of that." She lowered her voice. "That means there's another spy?"

"At least one more," Anya agreed. And if Nova Force was involved, this had to be related to the corporations somehow. It wasn't the first time they'd tried, but this was far more serious than Kade's recruitment or even Maggie and Jade's abduction. This time, they'd gone after the colonists themselves.

The conversation lulled as they all pondered what that meant. Then Maggie changed the subject. "How long until the new place is ready?"

"Not long. We approved the final plans yesterday." Anya grinned. "This time there will be two parcels of land—one for the shop and forge and another for our home."

"And given how much it seems to snow, this forge

will have a retractable roof to keep the weather out," Damos added.

Between bouts of lovemaking the three of them had talked about a wide variety of things, including business plans. The new place would be laid out properly, with room for all their work to be displayed. It was going to be part of a new market area, and it was only a short walk over the bridge to the tavern. Now that the rest of the human women were full members of the colony, they were all moving into the main settlement, clearing the way for the next batch of arrivals.

"Any word on when we're getting a human doctor?" Jade asked. "The healers here are amazing, but there's a lot they don't know about humans."

"They're recruiting right now. I haven't heard anything confirmed yet, but everyone on the council knows it's a priority."

Everything was a priority right now. They had to prepare for the new colonists from both Vardaria and Earth, secure this planet from any further attacks, and continue building Haven into a thriving community. Anya had come here looking for a new challenge. Now she had so much more than that. She had friends, family, love, and a home she'd fight to her last breath to defend.

Best of all, she had Damos and Tra'var. They'd gone from strangers to the best thing that had ever happened to her.

Her comms chimed and she stepped away from the conversation to answer it. It was her mother.

"Hey, little one. Sorry for the lack of communication. My comm array was on the fritz. So, how are things on Liberty? What did I miss?" Hezza's eyes narrowed as she stared through the screen at Anya. "And what the *fraxx* are those marks on your neck?"

~

Thank You for Reading Her Alien Forgemasters

Keep reading for a bonus scene from book four - Her Alien Spymaster

I hope you enjoyed Anya, Tra'var and Damos's story. If you're looking for more stories like this one, I invite you to explore the other books in the Drift universe, which now Include Haven Colony, Nova Force and the original Drift series.

BONUS SCENE

Yardan and Skye

Being sick was a new experience for Yardan, and he wasn't enjoying it. In fact, it was one of the most humiliating trials of his life. He was as weak as a newborn and his mind refused to focus. Worst of all, he needed to rely on other beings to help him. Even the simple act of relieving himself had left him exhausted.

The cyborg female, Skye, had carried him out of the tavern. Oh, he'd pretended she was just supporting him, but the truth was she'd barely let his feet touch the ground. He was grateful to her for not revealing just how weak he was, but he chafed at the thought that he now owed her for that sop to his already battered pride. He was the prince's trusted advisor, the one who unearthed every secret threat and stamped it out before it could take root. Not only had he failed to detect this attack, but he'd fallen victim to it himself, just like every other Vardarian in the colony.

He didn't have to open his eyes to know Skye was nearby. She'd stayed close ever since they'd returned to the prince's modest palace. "How's the prince?" he asked.

"Almost as grumpy as you are, but he's recovering quickly. You would be too if you'd taken the injection when it was first offered," she said wryly.

He opened his eyes and looked toward the sound of her voice. She sat less than a meter from his bedside. Her hair was somewhere between blonde and brown, darker now than it had been during the summer when the tips had been bleached by the sun. He'd seen her from a distance more than once, but they'd never spoken until yesterday. He had too much to do, and his position did not allow for distractions of any kind. Especially not females. A spymaster had but one purpose, and his loyalty to the one he served had to be absolute.

"I should have been given it first to ensure it was safe. Since no one thought to ask me, I saw no reason to put my need before that of the others in the prince's service."

She snorted. "You could just admit you were sulking because no one consulted you."

"I do not sulk. It would be beneath my station to behave in such a way."

"Uh huh." She gazed at him with eyes as blue as a summer sky. "I have spent my entire life surrounded by men who never want to admit to feeling emotions. You don't need to pretend with me."

He ignored her blunt statement to ask the question that had been foremost in his mind since his return to the palace. "Why are you even here?"

Her smile really was beguiling. It softened her features and made her seem approachable despite the fact she was far taller than most females and far more deadly. The cyborgs of the colony were all from the same research station, and every one of them had been deemed too dangerous to be allowed off world.

"Where else would I be?" she asked.

Answering a question with another question was one of his tricks, and he wasn't enjoying having it turned around on him. "That isn't an answer."

She cocked her head. "You haven't noticed yet? Breathe deeply, Yardan. Tell me what you smell."

He breathed in. His sense of smell was limited, but he could still pick up stronger odors. The scent of home cooking, the spikey tang of a suspect's fear... and even a whisper of something that shouldn't have been in his rooms—the scent of a female.

He shook his head. "I don't smell anything unusual, but that's not surprising. I haven't had full use of that sense in more years than I care to admit to."

Her smile flickered and then died. "What? Nothing? Why not?"

Yardan sat up, some sense whispering to him that this conversation was more important than he currently understood. "I am the prince's *Naram*

T'kar. You would call me his spymaster. The day I finished my training and made my vows, I did what all the others before me have done. Those in my role can have no distractions. I have no *anrik*. I severed ties to my family and friends. I gave up what few possessions I had, and the healers adjusted my senses so I will never be tempted by the greatest distraction of all."

"What would that be?" Her tone held a brittle edge now, and something wary and sad flickered in her lovely eyes. He had no idea why she was upset.

He touched his nose. "If I were to find my *mahaya*, I could not fulfill my duty. So the healers made me so that I cannot detect those pheromones. It affects my sense of smell and taste, too, but not completely."

"But how would that work? Even if you can't sense your mate, she would sense you."

"The ancestors set me on this path. I have no *mahaya*. But even if I did, the healers ensured I would never give off the pheromone that would attract a female."

Skye rose to her feet, tension crackling off her now. "You're wrong about that."

"I am not. This is my purpose. This is the life the ancestors set out for me when I was still a boy."

"Your ancestors got it wrong, then."

He didn't understand. "What did they get wrong?"

"You *do* have a *mahaya*, Yardan."

"That's not possible."

This time, her smile was bitter and sad. "Then why

have I been feeling the pull of the *sharhal* since I picked you up off that floor?"

"It's not. No. You can't be. I cannot have a mate."

"You're wrong about that."

"You don't understand. This isn't possible." It couldn't be. Not unless the ancestors had taken leave of their senses... or he wasn't supposed to be Tyran's spymaster anymore. Was he to be stripped of his position for failing to protect the prince? Was this some sort of punishment?

"You know, if you keep telling me I'm wrong and that you can't have a mate, I'm going to start taking it personally."

He scrubbed a hand over his close-cropped hair and tried to find some words that weren't going to make this situation worse. "It's not you. You're lovely. Truly. Any male would be lucky to claim you as his own. But I'm not that male. I can't be."

"You keep saying that." She walked over and put a callused hand on his cheek. "But you're wrong."

The touch of her hand felt better than anything he'd ever known. Tender. Gentle. Right.

He turned his head and brushed her hand away with his. "This is not happening."

"Oh, it is." She let her fingers graze over his cheek as she moved away. "If you don't believe me now, that's fine. I'll go to your healers and have them confirm it. Then I'm coming back here. You have until then to come to terms with this."

A tiny whisper of suspicion sounded at the back of

his mind. "You seem to be adjusting quite well to the idea of being bound to a stranger. Most humans take longer."

She winked at him. "I'm not human, though. I'm a cyborg. And after everything I've already survived in my life, this doesn't scare me at all. I've been to hell and back so many times I know the way blindfolded."

"And if I say no?" The words were out before he could stop himself. He knew what would happen if he denied her this claim. If it was real, that is. She'd suffer pain, madness, and possibly death.

"If you say no, that's your choice to make. I'd rather go back to hell again than take another being's choices away from them. I know too well how that feels."

He didn't know what to say to that, so he said nothing.

"There's one more thing I need to say, and then I'll go. Being stubborn is not the same as being right."

She blew him a kiss and departed, leaving him alone with dozens of questions and no answers.

Was the beautiful cyborg a planned distraction, a punishment... or his reward?

Want to know what happens next?
Her Alien Spymaster releases early in 2022

ABOUT THE AUTHOR

Susan lives out on the Canadian west coast surrounded by open water, dear family, and good friends. She's jumped out of perfectly good airplanes on purpose and accidentally swum with sharks on the Great Barrier Reef.

If the world ends, she plans to survive as the spunky, comedic sidekick to the heroes of the new world, because she's too damned short and out of shape to make it on her own for long.

You can find out more about Susan and her books at:
www.susanhayes.ca